THE FACES
OF MURDER

A Hightower Mystery
Book Two

By Marilyn Wright Dayton

#In this series /
Multi-murders on
a train in the
middle of the
desert — why
are the FBI and
a Russian mob
involved?

Enjoy!
Marilyn

The Faces of Murder is a work of fiction. Names, characters, places and incidents are the product of the author's imagination or are used fictitiously. Any resemblance to actual events, locales, or persons, living or dead is entirely coincidental.

Published through Amazon Kindle Direct Publishing

ISBN: 9798985320220

DEDICATION

I would like to dedicate this book to my family. Although I have had many challenges in my life, making many mistakes, they have always been supportive. I am in a place now, retired, where I can release all of those stories that have been in my head. And with the encouragement of my family and friends, this, my ninth book, is here.

I would also like to thank Patti "Nanny" Sweeney, my son-in-law's mother, who is an amazing gal. You see, as you get to know the characters in this book, especially the four gals from the nursing home who are spry and feisty, and who love mysteries, Patti and I could be two of them. Same age. Same feisty spirit.

And in that spirit, I continue this series, The Hightower Mysteries. I hope you enjoy this book, the second in the *Hightower Mystery Series*. It has been a long time coming, and when it began coming to me, it just flowed.

Marilyn
AUTHOR

CONTENTS

FACES OF MURDER

PREFACE

"As you know, life is an echo;
we get what we give."
- David DeNotaris

With each book in this series, we get to know our main characters better. We learn about their backgrounds, their personalities, and see how they act and react. The *'Cackle Gang'* is a unique blend of many personalities. When any of us gets older, in our early 70's, we figure out what it's *'all about'* and relax, being ourselves more than when we were younger. That's when we really become interesting *'characters'*.

In the Hightower Mystery Series, we read and learn how each *'gal becomes part of the whole'*, a gang that works together to solve some very complicated situations, like murder. As we read, watch, learn along with them, it is so easy to feel like we, ourselves, are members of the *'Cackle Gang'* too. So, come along on another adventure, dig in and enjoy!

Marilyn
AUTHOR

MAIN CHARACTERS

The "Cackle Gang" -
- Louise "Weezie" Hightower, retired P. I.
- Elizabeth "Bitsy Sutton retired dancer/actress
- Mildred "Millie" Swartout, grandmother
- Eleanor "Crip" Cripton, retired school teacher

Guy Davis, retired cop, security guard at Hightowers
Steward John Madden
The Police in Bahrump Junction, Nevada
- Police Chief Charles Passer
- His son Policeman Kevin Passer
- His nephew Policeman Karol Weiss
- Dr. Bookman, Medical Examiner

FBI Executive Director Bud Walsh
FBI Agents Willis & Mather
Gangster On Trial – Akim Ruizinho
- His wife is Alina Ruizinho
- His daughter is Sofia Ruizinho

Second Russian Crime Family - Sidorov
- Dmitriy Sidorov
- Maxim Volkov

Passengers of Note:
- Boris Lutoksky (Russian)
- Katherine Ruzinski (Russian-Polish)
- Detective At Large Harold W. Pinkton

The Victims -
- Victim No. One (Woman in her 40s)
- Victim No. Two (Teenage Girl)
- Victim No. Three (Man)

CHAPTER 1

THIS SMALL TOWN

"Everything negative – pressure, challenges – is all an opportunity for me to rise." - Kobe Bryant

The woman in the courthouse was waiting for the elevator. It stopped and the door opened. She stood tall with medium brown skin and amazing eyes, which at the moment wore a puzzled look.

Before her on the elevator were two men, each holding bowls with the contents of their pockets. The men were handcuffed together. She looked down at the bowls where on the top lay the men's badges. She looked up at them. *"Okay, which one is the arrestor, and which is the arrestee?"*

They looked at her and smiled, *"That is debatable,"* said one. The other one added, *"Depends on which team wins today."* And they smiled. Small towns, gotta love them.

The two men were cousins, growing up together in this town, as close as brothers. Everyone who knew them (well that would be the whole town), knew how they loved to play games and jokes with one another, so this latest wasn't surprising.

When the woman left the elevator, the two looked at one another and smiled. They were each thinking, *'Got her.'*

Then both of their cell phones went off. At the same time. With the same sound…a special alert. Their smiles faded, replaced with determination and questions. They thought the same thing, *"Well, that means something big. Time to get serious."*

By the time they got to the police offices on the fifth floor, their bowls were empty, their pockets were stuffed, and their facial expressions were serious; and they looked focused. They were police officers once again, intent on finding out what the big emergency was. They walked into the Chief of Police's office, who happened to be one's father, and the other's uncle.

"*Well boys, we got something going on, and it's about to roll into town,*" said the Police Chief. "*I want you to help them out. Seems like there has been some kind of murder on the train.*" At their questioning faces, he clarified, "*You know, the train that usually blows through here, because we are some kind of 'no-name small town' that doesn't count, and isn't listed on their itinerary?*" He was answered with two nods.

"*Yup, that one. The cross-country train. Well, this time they ARE stopping, and will probably be staying for a while. Boys, we got ourselves a murder to solve. Get down to the train station, get on that train, and make sure it stays here so we can do that. Okay?*"

Two more nods, and they were off. The Chief yelled after them, "*Good luck, boys, and keep me in the loop.*"

CHAPTER 2

ON THE TRAIN – TWO DAYS BEFORE

"There is something in a person's eyes that you cannot see anywhere else in the world. Something haunting and unsettling." - Anonymous

Millie was watching the young girl closely, staring at her actually.

"Millie, what are you doing?" whispered Weezie.

"There is something odd about that girl that just doesn't feel right," she replied.

"It's not nice to stare," added Bitsy.

The three elderly women were traveling together on an adventure, riding the train across North America from California to New York City. They had flown from NYC to California for a few days. Their favorite destination had been the NAPA Valley, where the three had enjoyed different types of white wine. For them, a trip to '*heaven*'. Now, they were ready to head home and slowly travel by rail to see the country.

They were in their early 70's and lived together in a senior living facility in Upstate New York. Millie was a stay-at-home mother-grandmother all of her life. Bitsy was a retired actress-dancer. And Weezie was a retired Private Investigator, who had returned just a few months earlier from solving a murder case in Arizona.

Millie couldn't help but watch two women who were seated

across the aisle. The younger one looked to be a teenager, wearing no makeup, fairly petite. She kept her face downward as if shy. Or '*maybe hiding?*' wondered Millie. She couldn't seem to take her eyes off the girl. When she looked over at the woman who was traveling with the girl, Millie noticed something about her too. Her face was pretty, but she had '*stiff*' features, that didn't seem to change at all. Like a human mask. '*Strange',* she thought. '*Botox??*'" Then the woman noticed Millie staring, and Millie looked away, and out the window. She saw that they were now traveling through Nevada. The land was fairly flat and dry, several shades of brown. She knew they would soon be in Reno, the Biggest Little City in the World,

After waiting a few minutes, Millie looked back over at the two. She noticed that they had risen and were walking away. '*Maybe to the bathroom?*' she thought. Millie really couldn't put her finger on what was so different about those two. She knew it was '*something*', but what?

Mildred "Millie" Swartout was usually the one who calmed everyone else down, acting like the grandmother that she was. But this time, she couldn't seem to calm her own thoughts down. She tried to look out the window and concentrate on the scenery again.

The thought that '*Something doesn't feel right about them,*' stayed in her mind. Little did Millie know that she would be one of the last people to see those two women alive.

CHAPTER 3

THE FOURTH GAL

"Curiosity about life in all of its aspects, I think, is still the secret of great creative people."
- Leo Burnett

After dinner, the three gals gathered together in one of their sleepers to call the fourth member of their '*Cackle Gang*', Crip. Eleanor "Crip" Cripton had to stay behind, missing their train trip, due to illness. She was recovering from hip replacement surgery, a major surgery, especially when you are paralyzed from the waist down as Crip was. Even though she was in a wheelchair, she was still an actively involved member of the '*Gang*', helping to solve mysteries that came their way, which is often the case. During closer testing, it was also discovered that Crip suffered from Multiple Sclerosis, a degenerative and disabling disease of the brain and spinal cord (central nervous system). Her doctors had yet to make a decision on treatment for her MS, first waiting until she was recovered from her hip surgery. '*One thing at a time,*' Millie had said.

The three girls had also thought that Crip would have balked at coming with them on a train journey, thinking that her being confined to a wheelchair would limit any activities they may have wanted to do. But they really didn't care about that and would have done everything they could to make the trip enjoyable for their good friend, wheelchair or not.

"Hey, Crip, what's up?" asked Bitsy. Bitsy, although in her early 70s, was young at heart, and acted it too, a great deal of the time, '*over-acting*' as Crip had often said. They all loved her anyway.

Crip laughed, a sound they loved to hear, especially given her health situation. *"I'm doing great! Usually, after surgery, they have you get up and walk 400 steps within the first 24 hours. Couldn't quite do that,"* she continued to laugh.

Weezie jumped into the conversation, *"Crip, tell us how you feel...and what was it like? Did you have any reactions to the pain meds they had given you?"*

"Oh, you know me. I asked for the strongest they had, even asked if weed would help." Again, the laughter.

Millie joined in, *"Crip, tell me. Have you ever smoked that stuff? Every once in a while, you joke about it, wondering out loud if you should have it as part of your treatment. So, have you?"*

"Well...not exactly. I had friends who used to swear by it, for when you have pain. And, of course, sometimes when you don't". Again laughing.

Millie actually snorted when she laughed. *"Crip, you tear me up! But seriously, I'm so sorry we were in California sipping wine when they decided to operate. We all wish we had been there. And you know, we could have cut short our trip, finishing it another time..."*

"NO!" Crip jumped right in. *"You girls have nothing to feel guilty about. Besides Guy has been here beside me all the time. He is just so great with the medical team. I don't know where he has learned so much, knowing the right questions to ask and all that."*

The girls were quiet for a moment. *"Crip, remember that his wife was sick for a couple of years before she died. I guess you could say, he learned a lot then."* Weezie was remembering how Guy Davis, a retired detective and currently head of security at their senior facility, had shared the story with them a couple of years before.

The girls were quiet again.

Millie picked up the conversation, not wanting the sad feelings to transfer through the line to Crip. "*So, no weed, Crip. But are you in pain at all?*"

"*Well, yes, just a bit. It's under control though. Even though I can't really feel much below my waist, I can feel an ache in my hip area, that's all. Curious, isn't it? I certainly didn't expect to be able to feel anything really.*" Then, she laughed again, "*Tell me girls, have you met any gorgeous men yet?*"

"*Oh, my God, girl,*" responded Bitsy. "*Actually, we have seen some, but not met any…sad to say.*" Bitsy loved to flirt with men…anyone, anywhere. That was just part of who she was.

"*All of this aside, Crip, we have been praying for your recovery. We want to be able to do something special when we get back to help celebrate that you are doing so well,*" said Weezie. "*And, of course, to thank Guy, he would have to be part of it too. That man is very special, and I think he really has come to love us. I don't know what I would have done on that murder case a few months ago, if he hadn't been there with me. He was absolutely a life saver, and quite the mystery solver.*"

The girls all agreed, and Millie said, "*I think we should make it official…he can become the only male member of our 'Cackle Gang'. What do you think, girls?*"

Again, that marvelous sound of laughter that only women who have lived through a lot of pain in their lives can make…full gut involvement, loud and raucous. Crip handled everything in her life as if it wasn't a big deal. She had once said to them, "*Look at life as a swimming pool. Whether you immerse yourself into the shallow end or into the deep end, you still get wet.*"

Millie picked up the conversation. "*Guess what, Crip? I happened to notice something a bit mysterious on our train ride today. There are two women, they look like a mother and her* teenaged daughter. Although I feel there is something a bit off about them. I just can't put my finger on it, but it's definitely not normal"

"Oh, I wonder what is going to happen? Maybe they are in disguise? Maybe they are mass murderers. Or maybe they are escaping from some horrible event, or running away from something or someone?" Crip responded.

Weezie cut that short, "Come on, girls. None of that. We don't want to have a murder or a mystery on our trip. We are here to relax, see the country, and have a bit of fun."

"Yeah, I want to learn how to line dance. Maybe when we get to Reno, there might be a country bar where we could do that?" joined in Bitsy.

The girls groaned.

Hearing a yawn over the phone from Crip, the girls decided to finish their phone call. Wishing a lot of love to one and all, and continued prayers and hugs to Crip, they signed off. Then they each went to their sleeper cabins. The only one who didn't sleep well that night was Millie. She couldn't get the two women out of her mind. She decided she would approach them in the morning at breakfast, introduce herself, and get to know them a little. Maybe her imagination was just running overtime.

CHAPTER 4

WHERE ARE THEY?

"There are no regrets in life, just lessons."
- Jennifer Aniston

Early the next morning, the girls met for breakfast, hoping to get a full day in of exploring Reno, Nevada. The train had pulled into the station, parking on a side rail for the day.

Millie kept looking around the dining car. *"I don't see them. You know, those two women…mother and daughter…whatever. I was hoping to meet them."* She turned to the other two gals, *"It kept me up a large part of the night, with scenarios going thru my mind. I think Crip was right, even though she was sort of kidding around with it, you know? Those two women are running away from something…someone…I don't know. There is definitely something going on. They looked like they were trying to hide their faces or something, each time I looked over at them. Who are they?"* And she looked around the car, *"And where are they?"*

Weezie decided to try to nip this in the bud, *"Millie, we are on a trip. We have an entire day ahead of us to see Reno. Maybe they have already gotten off the train. Maybe they are sleeping in. I don't know…and I don't care!"* She got up, having finished eating, *"And right now, I am itching to see Reno. I even want to try some of their slot machines."* She looked down at the girls, *"They have those, don't they?"*

Millie got out the brochure the train company had provided, and read out loud, while Weezie sat back down for a moment. *"Here is some information from this tour brochure. This one says 'The best way to see all that Downtown Reno has to offer! On this*

30-45 minute tour, you will see the Reno Strip, Murals, the famous Truckee River and Riverwalk, Wingfield Park, and BOTH of the Reno Arches! Your experienced tour guide will give you fun information about the history of Reno and the Truckee River.' The only problem with that tour is you go around in cars and it is limited to two people per car."

Weezie added, "Remember, girls, we have already signed up for the audio tour of Reno," and she reached over to point to where it was listed in the brochure, "'Weave through the different periods of Reno's boom and bust on this self-guided audio tour of the downtown area. Reno, with its highs as a glitzy desert town filled with cowboys and celebrities, to its lows as a washed-up gambling town and the butt of many jokes on late night TV, has never failed to keep America fascinated. It's a contradictory place that rides high and dips low. And, as it turns out, that oscillation was built into the city's character from the beginning. This walking tour starts at Reno's Arch'. Oh, I think that sounds like such fun!"

"That does sound like fun," added Bitsy. "But what about those scavenger hunts they have? They have like half a dozen of them."

"Didn't you want to be available for a dinner and fun in the late afternoon? That means one long tour around Reno, then we head to that, no time for scavenger tours," added in Millie.

"So, where are we going to go for eating and fun?" asked Bitsy.

Millie sighed, because this ditsy friend of theirs has such a short memory and has forgotten what they had talked about days ago. "Okay, Bitsy, here is the plan we agreed on, remember? We decided to eat at one of the Steakhouses, then go to the Country Western bar where you wanted to dance. It is actually located inside one of their larger casinos, and I think it was called The Cowboys Chance…or something like that. Remember??"

Bitsy frowned, a look that didn't look very good on her

overly-made-up face, "*Yea, I think so. Well, anyway, let's get going. We need to get off this train…the space is just too tight to move in here.*"

Weezie laughed, *"Plus you can't really dance around in here, can you, Bitsy?"* They all laughed, even Bitsy.

Still in her mind, Millie was wondering where those two women were. The only place to leave the train was here in Reno, and then not again until Chicago. If they did get off, she hoped that they wouldn't miss getting back on. She really couldn't shake her need to find them and meet them. So many questions in her head…

CHAPTER 5

FINDING THE BODIES

"Get busy living or get busy dying.." – Steven King

Millie needn't have worried, as she would get to see the two women again. Not to meet them, but to '*witness*' them.

That same night, they saw some people running late to the train after their Reno adventures. Being an observant type of gal, Millie laughed as she shared, *"Looks like some quite interesting people are on this train. I doubt we will be bored on our way cross country."*

After everyone was back on board, as the train began moving eastward, the girls were sitting looking out the window at the passing scenery. Millie particularly noticed a rather mismatched couple. Millie would never have thought to put them together. He was short, stocky with stringy hair that needed a good washing. His suit seemed at least a decade old, needing a pressing. She was tall, thin and stately looking with long luxurious dark hair and flashing dark eyes. And those dark eyes were flashing at the man beside her. The woman rose quickly and purposely leaving him looking fairly confused. At least he was smart enough to read the signs and stayed where he was, sitting alone with a confused, almost blank look on his face.

Since she was feeling a bit restless, Millie went for a short walk, along one of the hallways in the sleeper car. She happened to notice a large stain coming out from under one of the sleeper cabins, and a strange smell emanating from that cabin.

Because it seemed rather suspicious, she brought it to the

attention of one of the stewards, who made a call to his boss for permission to investigate. So, when the steward went to check that cabin, Millie decided to go with him. After a knock and no answer, he found his master key and opened the door. Millie began screaming. There was a lot of blood…it seemed to be everywhere. And two bodies, the two women…dead.

The steward closed the door, and they moved away, back to the phone where he could make another call.

The steward's boss decided to stop the train in the next town and contact the police there. The small town was basically in the middle of nowhere, set in the desert…an unscheduled stop. He estimated they would arrive there by morning.

CHAPTER 6

STOP THE TRAIN!

"If life were predictable, it would cease to be life, and be without flavor." – Eleanor Roosevelt

It didn't take long for the rumors to spread through the train. Word got back to the Cackle Gang through Millie, who was the first to suggest *"Weezie, you are a private eye, with years of experience solving crimes. You need to tell the steward, or whoever, that you can help them."*

Weezie was tempted, and when the girls pushed a little harder, she decided to do just that. The steward was happy to hear that she could help and quickly deferred to her. He took her to see the cabin and the victims. Weezie noticed that the poor man looked very pale and seemed to be sweating heavily. She was sure that he had never seen a crime scene before.

So, she told him she would go ahead and look, and he could go about his work or simply stand somewhere out in the corridor if he preferred. He nodded, and when they got to the cabin, he backed away several cabins down the hall to where the smell wasn't as noticeable. Because of the murder and the smell, the stewards had moved those from the cabins on wither side and across the hallway to different cabins. Thank heavens there were several available that had been empty.

As she began to open the cabin door, Weezie was interrupted by a man who approached her, flashed a badge, identifying himself as a detective. She didn't get that close of a at the badge but decided to let him in with the idea that she could watch him closely. She hoped he wasn't flashing a bogus badge.

Weezie asked him if he could take notes as would she, in case one of them might miss something the other didn't. All he said when he looked inside the cabin was *"Hmmm."* He didn't look surprised at who the two women were, as if he *'had been expecting it??'* Weezie felt a bit confused, wondering what was going on with this man and exactly who he really was. Did he know the victims? When she looked closely at him, almost staring, he began to act nervous, and slowly began to back away from her. She asked him if she should lead the investigation, and he nodded, staying where he was, in the doorway.

She began to focus on the scene. She wrote down in her notebook the first things she noticed which were:

- The older woman (40-ish perhaps) looked familiar.
- The younger female (teenager perhaps) didn't.
- They had both been shot, one shot each, right in the heart
- Then they had their throats slashed.
- Upon closer inspection, she looked along their jaw lines and behind their ears…both had recent facial reconstructive surgery…meaning what? Faked IDs?
- There was absolutely NO identification anywhere in the cabin, and only two small suitcases, with just clothes and toiletries…no paperwork, no wallets, nothing to tell her who they were.
- Was this a robbery gone wrong? Or something else?

She wondered where they had gotten on the train, and started a list to ask the steward, or at least to have him find the answers to.

She noticed that the so-called detective had come closer and was about to lean onto the upper bunk edge, so he could get a closer look at the victims. She stopped him, pushing him back, *"Don't touch anything. There will be fingerprints we need to check out…I think we are done here."* And she pushed him out and closed the door behind them. She did not like this man, whoever he was.

CHAPTER 7

WHAT HAPPENED?

"Life is really simple, but men insist on making it complicated."
- Confucius

Steward John Madden has heard a lot of jokes about his name, people asking him if he was retired from coaching football, and other fairly insulting comments. Over the years, he had learned to keep his head down and forge ahead, shutting out all of those unimportant comments.

Today, he had a difficult job to do. Once he had been able to pull himself together after finding two dead bodies in the cabin, and clearing his nose of the smells, he gathered some yellow police tape, marveling at *'why would they have some of this on a train? Maybe crime happens often on trains??'* At any rate, he focused again, and set about placing the tape over the doorway to the cabin, then standing watch over it for as long as he needed to. He was determined not to let anyone mess up his crime scene, except the nice retired P.I. lady and the detective.

He knew that as soon as they pulled into the train station, the local police would be taking over, and his job would be done. Until then, he stood tall, proud to be the one responsible for *'protecting' those poor women murdered in their cabin'*. Then he had another thought, *'That means there is a murderer on this train.'* And he felt shivers that shook him to the core. Never knowingly had he been this close to murder scenes nor murderers. He couldn't wait for the train to stop at the next town.

Meanwhile, Weezie had decided to have a talk with this so-called detective. They had already told everyone that all passengers needed to return to their cabins until it was time to question them. There were, of course, a lot of complaints, the loudest being her friends, Millie and Bitsy. She didn't want to even think about that, the girls would get over it. Plus, they knew that Weezie would share anything she learned with them. After all, they were a '*crime solving team*'. At least in their minds.

So, Detective At Large Harold W. Pinkton sat down with Weezie in the dining car to discuss the murder. She asked again to see his badge. '*Hm, interesting,*' she thought to herself. Then she asked him, "*What does 'Detective At Large' mean, Mr. Pinkton?*"

He chuckled, "*Well, little lady. I am retired too. So, I 'rent' myself out to those who are in need of detective work. That could be anything from researching a case, solving a case, to protecting a suspect or a witness.*"

"*And which is it this time?*"

"*Well, I guess I'll need to tell you. I was hired to watch over these two little ladies that were killed.*"

"*Great job, Mr. Pinkton.*"

"*No need to be mean about it, I did watch over them. I couldn't exactly go into their cabin and watch them sleep, now, could I?*"

Weezie shrugged her shoulders. "*Were you stationed outside their cabin door to prevent anyone from going in and killing them?*"

Detective-At-Large Harold W. Pinkton turned pale. "*Well, not exactly. I decided to spend the night in my cabin, then return in the morning. I really didn't think they were in that much danger."*

"You didn't?" Weezie asked him, feeling irritated. *"You do know who they were, don't you?"*

"Well, I wouldn't exactly say I knew who they really were."

Weezie sat straighter in her seat and took a sip of her hot tea. *"I'll tell you who they were NOT, Mr. Pinkton. They were NOT who they appeared to be."*

He gave her a blank look…waiting.

"I'm not sure just how much I can trust you, sir, because I don't think you are very good at your job. But, in confidence, as I have no choice, as we are apparently teaming up on this case, they were NOT Alina and Sofia Ruizinho."

Mr. Pinkton's face turned a paler shade of white, if that was even possible. And he began to sweat, quite heavily. *"What do you mean, they weren't them?"*

"I think I have said enough for now. When the police come on board from the small town we plan to stop at, you may overhear my explanation to them. For now, I'm just not ready to trust you with everything I found. Sorry, but that's the way I feel."

Pinkton gave her a sly smile, *"Well, well, little lady. You sure are good at keeping secrets."*

Weezie returned his sly smile, *"That's what people have been paying me to do for several decades. Now if you will excuse me, I think we are slowing down. I want to be ready along with Steward Madden for the police."* And she rose, *"You can do what you wish for now, but stay where I can easily find you."* And she walked away.

They were indeed slowing down, preparing to stop at the station, and then be guided to a side rail where they would be able to park the train for a few days.

The two policemen were waiting for them on the platform, climbed onto the train, directing the engineer to the side rail where they would be out of the way of any other trains that may pass through. Very rarely do they have any trains stop in their town.

The policemen then walked to the dining car to find someone to talk to. Weezie had relieved Steward Madden so that Madden could meet the police there and direct them to the crime scene. She stood outside the victims' cabin door.

As the police (guided by Steward Madden) approached Weezie, they looked at one another, smiled, and one reached out his hand to introduce himself to her. "*How are you, ma'am? I am Kevin Passer, and welcome to Bahrump Junction! This is my fellow policeman Karol Weiss. And who might you be?*"

Steward Madden stepped forward, "*Gentlemen, I would like to introduce you to a renowned Private Investigator Weezie Hightower. We are very lucky that she was on our train and was able to help protect our crime scene; and she knew exactly what to do. Otherwise, we would have been floundering here.*"

The two policemen smiled out of respect nodding their heads to her, "*Pleasure ma'am.*"

Weezie smiled back at them and took a breath to begin filling them in on what happened. Before she could say anything, Detective Pinkton appeared and stepped in front of her, flashing his badge. "*Gentlemen, I am working alongside Ms. Hightower on this case. I would be happy to answer any questions you may have.*"

Policeman Passer looked closely at the badge, asking

"What does this mean, Detective At Large? I've never heard of that." He looked up at the detective with a stern look, *"Does that mean you sell yourself out to the highest bidder on cases?"*

Pinkton flushed, quite a contrast to the previous ashen face he had been wearing a short time before. *"Why, sir, I am a trustworthy detective of many decades, and was hired to protect the slain women."*

Passer continued his stern look, *"Well, it would seem that you didn't do your job very well this time. I think we can work with Ms. Hightower on this, and you can sit in the dining car and await any questions we may have for you."*

And he turned to the cabin door, ready to view the crime scene, ignoring Pinkton completely. Pinkton slinked away, mumbling to himself. Weezie smiled to herself. *'Good for you, young man,'* she thought.

Weezie proceeded to step forward, moving the yellow tape aside, and opened the door slightly. She turned to the two young policemen, not knowing how much experience they may have had at viewing dead bodies. *"Are you ready?"* They both nodded.

When she opened the door, exposing the full extent of the slaughter of the women, the young men confirmed by their expressions that they had indeed never witnessed such a scene.

So, Weezie tried to distract them with some facts about the murder. *"There are two female victims, one aged in her early 40s, the other a girl in her late teens, perhaps 19. They have been shot, just once each, at close proximity, in the heart, then their throats were slashed, to finish the job...which was unnecessary, as I am sure both women were already dead. Otherwise, there would have been even more blood."* Then she paused, wondering if these two young men were going to be able to proceed.

FACES OF MURDER

Policeman Passer asked her, *"Do you mean, there could have been more blood than we see here?"*

Weezie smiled at him, impressed at his interest in learning, *"Why, yes, there would have been. When your heart is stopped, it no longer pumps blood out to the body, so there is a kind of 'overflow' of the blood from the wound. Also, around the neck area, there is minimal overflow. Otherwise, blood would have splattered all over the walls and cots."*

"I see," he said as he swallowed with difficulty. *"What else can you tell us?"*

"I took a close look at their faces, and it was as I suspected. They both had facial surgery, fairly recently, to change their looks. And in this case, it was to make them look like two other women."

Both of the policemen looked confused. Policeman Weiss spoke up, *"Why would they want to look like two other women? What two women? Who were they made to look like? I'm sure you know? And was there any ID in their cases to help us?"*

"Why, no to the IDs...nothing anywhere, and yes, I do know who they were supposed to look like. You might recognize the name. They were made to look like a mother and daughter, Alina and Sofia Ruizinho." She waited to see if they would recognize the names. And they did.

The two men looked at one another, Passer spoke, *"Do you mean the wife and daughter of the Russian mobster Akim Ruizinho, who is awaiting trial? Weren't they supposed to be witnesses for the prosecution, telling what they knew about the illegal activities of the man and his organization?"*

"Exactly."

"*Well then, why were these two made to look like those two witnesses, and what were they doing on this train? And by the way, where would the real wife and daughter be?*"

"*Those are good questions. And at this time, I don't have the answers. But I have a suggestion about how we can find out. I will share that with you in a moment. First, I want to draw your attention to the fingerprints…the bloody fingerprints on the rail of the top bunk,*" and she pointed to them. "*I think the killer actually leaned there as he or she was cutting their throats, unnecessarily of course. We need to get fingerprints of everyone on this train, passengers and personnel. Can we get a forensic person here to help us?*"

Policeman Passer stood straight and said, "*Of course. We have a forensic person as well as a medical examiner. I am going to send my cousin, er, Policeman Weiss back to the station to round them up.*" He turned to him and sent him off to do just that.

"*Ms. Hightower, what is your suggestion on how we can find out more about this case and answers to our questions?*"

Weezie smiled, "*I know someone. Could I use your phone? I can't seem to get a good enough signal for my own cell.*"

Passer smiled back at her, "*Aha, calling in the big wigs, eh? Who would that be…CIA or FBI?*"

Weezie winked at him, "*Why yes, that would be the FBI.*"

CHAPTER 8

WHO ARE THESE PEOPLE?

*"Identity is a prison you can never escape, but the way
to redeem your past is not to run from it, but
to try to understand it, and use it as a foundation
to grow.." – Jay-Z*

Weezie needed somewhere quiet and private to call her friend in the FBI. Actually, that friend was an Executive Director, someone she has known for several decades, ever since she met him on one of her cases when he was called in as a government consultant. He had been a young man fresh from Quantico. He stayed *'green'* only for a short time. Weezie and her husband taught him a lot on that particular case. And he has always been grateful. They had also worked on other cases together over the years. And right now, she needed him to give her some answers. Or at least find those answers for her.

Executive Director Walsh was in a meeting when she called. But when his secretary heard Weezie's name, she knew to interrupt him. When he came on the line, he sounded delighted to hear Weezie's voice. *"What in tarnation brings you to call me, Weezie gal?"* He was originally from Texas and never quite lost his drawl, nor his Texas manner of speaking.

He always made Weezie smile when she heard his voice, remembering how eager he had been when they first met, fresh faced and speaking so straight-forwardly, and typically Texan. *"Well, Bud, we have a murder here on a train in the middle of the desert in Nevada. Two women, one 40-ish and one late-teens, who have recently had a facial makeover to look like Alina and*

Sofia Ruizinho. Would you happen to know anything about them?"

"Oh, boy. Dead are they?"

"As a door-nail."

"Okay. Yes, I know about it. They were supposed to be decoys, to pull the attention of the mob and their friends away from where we have stashed the real ones….DAMN! It worked too well, I guess. Looks like we'll need to increase our protection for the real mother and daughter and move them again. DAMN!"

"Do you want to be involved here?"

"Yes, we do. I have two special agents who are on top of this case, and I will send them to you. I need your exact location. These guys will also bring you a file to review. As far as it goes, you are a member of our little FBI family, and we can trust you. But just don't let anyone get their hands on the file, okay?"

"Of course, Bud. When will they get here?"

"Not for at least 24 hours. Meanwhile, Weezie, I'm sure you have good control over this crime scene. Now, where exactly are you?"

"Well, Bud, we are parked on a railroad track by a very small town, one you probably never heard of. It's called Bahrump Junction, Nevada."

"What's that again??"

Weezie repeated it, laughing. *"Would you like me to spell it for you?"*

"Nope. I just found it in our database. Small is right. Okay, there is a Police Chief there named Charles Passer. I am going to

contact him and let him know that you will be handling this investigation on our behalf. And that two agents will be there within 24 hours to help you. And I repeat, Weezie…'to help you'. I know how you work, and I want you to solve this. And you call me on my cell next time with updates, okay? Not the office line. My cell is secure too."

"I definitely will, Bud. Thank you for your confidence in me."

"Confidence, shmay-fidence…I know you will solve this. And, believe me, this is a BIG one. I think you may have at least two people, maybe more, as riders on that train, who are there representing the Russian Mob. And I bet you anything they killed those poor gals."

"Bud, I will do my best to find them. Do you have anyone on this train that was supposed to protect them?"

"Yes, but she is working undercover, and we need to keep that close to our chests. When the time is right, she will step forward."

"A woman? I thought maybe you had meant a man. We have a so-called 'Detective For Hire' here named Pinkton who claims to have been hired by you to protect them."

"Never heard of him. I will research him and get back to you, okay? And anything else happens…anything…you call me, okay?"

"You've got it, Bud. Talk soon…and thanks."

"Be careful, woman. I wouldn't want anything to happen to you, okay? Stay close to both the police and the agents once they get there. Promise?"

"Promise." When she signed off, she looked around her

cabin, giving her the quiet she needed to think about this case. First on her agenda was to talk with the so-called *'Detective At Large'* Pinkton. Who the devil is he??

CHAPTER 9

ANOTHER BODY??

"You must expect great things of yourself before you can do them." – Michael Jordan

Weezie stopped at the dining car, looking for Pinkton, but didn't see him anywhere. It had been a couple of hours since she had seen him at the crime scene, and she thought perhaps he had been feeling rejected and *'went to his room/cabin'* like a spoiled child. She noticed there was no one in the dining car even though it was the dinner hour. Perhaps the police preferred everyone to stay in their cabins and order dinner trays. Probably a good idea.

But first, she stopped by the crime scene, where the door was once again closed, with Steward Madden standing in guard. *"Have you seen the police or are they still inside the cabin?"* she asked Madden.

"No, they said something about looking over the passenger lists and waiting for their medical examiner before removing the bodies. I don't know exactly where they are right now. Is there something I can do?"

Weezie smiled at him, *"No, that's fine. You have been so very helpful, I appreciate it. I think I need to have a talk with the Detective At Large Pinkton. Do you know which cabin is his?"*

When Steward Madden gave her the information, she headed off in that direction, unaware that this case was going to get even more complicated when she got to Pinkton's cabin.

Her cell phone rang, and she saw that it was Millie. She

decided to stop by Millie's cabin and quickly fill the gals in before they exploded the phone lines trying to reach her. She knew that her friends would literally prowl the halls of the train looking for her if she didn't talk with them soon.

Millie answered her door with a stern look, *"What is going on, Weezie? We have been told to stay in our cabins and just wait…it seems forever! Bitsy is here with me, come in and please tell us what's happening!"*

Weezie smiled at the girls, then changed her expression to a more serious look. *"Ladies, we have quite a development here."* And she began to pace in what little space there was to do that. *"Something is going on here that is beyond me, and I had to call my friend Bud at the FBI."*

The gals leaned forward, waiting. Bitsy opened her mouth about to say something when Weezie held up her hand. *"I can't tell you everything right now, but I can say that these two females were not who they seemed to be. Millie, you were right."*

Millie would have liked to say that she *'had tried to tell them',* but somehow didn't feel like saying anything. So, she waited for more from Weezie.

"These two women had facial reconstructive surgery and were supposed to be decoys for two women who were involved with the Russian mob. The real women are in hiding and being protected by the government, specifically the FBI." And Weezie sat down beside Millie, leaning her head on the woman's shoulder. *"I'm getting too old for this. I feel exhausted."*

Millie put her arms around Weezie's shoulders, *"No, my dear, you just feel a bit overwhelmed right now. Don't worry, your brain will keep you moving ahead on this case. This is what you were meant to do, and you know that. You solve mysteries, that's who you are. You may be trying to be retired, but I don't think you ever really will be."* She paused for effect, *"And it's OK to feel exhausted. You have had quite a day. Our dinner is about to arrive, want to share some of it? You really should eat something. That will help give you the energy to 'get back at it'."* And Millie smiled at Weezie.

Weezie smiled back at her, *"You are really quite wonderful, you know that, Millie?" You are the world's best mother, grandmother, and friend…to us all."* As she looked over at Bitsy.. *"You are our calming force. You balance us out, with me being 'brain drained', and Bitsy being, well…Bitsy."* And she smiled. The two gals smiled back at her.

Weezie stood up, *"I think I will grab something to eat from the kitchen first, then find our missing Detective At Large. That man needs to explain just exactly who he is. The FBI doesn't know him, and definitely didn't hire him. I really think he may be a larger part of this than I originally thought."*

As she walked to the door, she looked back at her two friends. *"Ladies, thank you, as always, for being there for me. I feel better already. If I don't see you before you go to bed, get a good night's sleep, I think tomorrow is going to be very busy. And I could really use your help tomorrow. Night."* And she left the cabin.

The kitchen staff acted as if they knew she was in charge of the murder case and were more than happy to give her some dinner. They watched her as she quietly ate right there in the kitchen, wanting to ask her questions, but somehow knowing they weren't permitted to. They just stood quietly for a few minutes until she reminded them that there were other hungry people on the train too. She said it with a smile, of course. That seemed to break their silence, and they got back to their work, all talking at once.

When she finished, she took a deep breath, feeling a bit better, and made her way to Pinkton's cabin. On her way, she met Policeman Passer, who joined her.

When there was no answer to her knocking, Passer was able to open the cabin door, as he had gotten a master set of cabin keys from Steward Madden. What they found took their breath away.

Pinkton lay dead in the middle of his cabin, stabbed once in the heart, blood pooled under his body. Both Weezie and Passer stood there in shock for a moment, until they both snapped out of it and began investigating the body and cabin like the professionals they were.

As they were checking out Pinkton's pockets in his jacket, Weezie told Passer what the FBI had said about not knowing this Detective At Large. When Passer pulled out a wad of cash from one of the inside jacket pockets, they looked at one another, saying out loud, *"Where did this man get all of this money? And why?"*

There were no other clues in the cabin, and as Passer called in to his office to report the second crime, Weezie began to recap everything in her mind, closing her eyes as she did.

'Pinkton was an overweight and rather slovenly character, whose clothes showed that he didn't have very much money. Yet, he had $10,000 in his coat pocket. No blood on the money…which means…what?? Was this a setup or did this man actually earn this money somehow? Did he murder the two women? Did he take money from their cabin somehow? Was he hired by the mob??'

Weezie held her head in her hands, overwhelmed by it all. Yup, she was definitely not as young as she used to be. She could have worked on this all night if she were even ten years younger. Those days are gone. And she now needed some sleep.

Passer told her he would take care of the three bodies, and make up a second copy of his notes for her so they could discuss everything first thing in the morning over some strong coffee.

Weezie was so grateful, left it all in his hands, and fell

asleep in her cabin fully clothed. She was '*done for the day.*'

CHAPTER 10

LOOKING FOR CLUES

*"Life imposes things on you that you can't control, but
You still have the choice of how you're going to live through."*
- Celine Dion

The next morning, Weezie should have felt rested, but she felt achy and hurt...everywhere. *"Damn,"* she said out loud. *"I'm just getting too old for all of this."* And she sighed, reflecting, *"Well, at least my brain is still working. Can't say much for this poor old body, which really feels its age...ugh!"* Then she noticed that she was still dressed, and on top of the covers. She laughed! Loudly. And she changed her mind, *"Oh, how this brings back memories...falling onto the bed to try to get some rest before getting back up to work on a case. I have really missed that."* And another huge laugh. She rose off the covers, but very slowly.

Once she had a shower to try to revive those *'old bones'* and dressed in new clothes, she headed to the dining car. By the time she arrived there, just the simple act of moving her body had helped make those aches and pains better. After taking another deep breath, she was ready...for whatever this new day would bring.

Waiting for her were Millie and Bitsy at one table, and the two policemen at another. She smiled at the gals, but moved on to sit with the police, as they had risen in anticipation of her joining them. They looked at her as if they had news for her. And so they did.

Passer was the first to speak, *"We already have initial autopsy news on the two women. And another one coming in as soon as they are done with the man."*

"What do you have to share about the women?"

Passer smiled, *"You were right. They had recent surgery on their faces, and we are waiting for the database to give us their identities, based on their fingerprints."*

Weezie didn't want to burst their bubble, because she knew that the FBI already had the women's identities, as they were the ones who had hired the two women to look like the witnesses. So, she simply waited, smiling. *"Anything special about them? Were they healthy?"*

"Yes, it seems there were no health problems with either of them. Nothing outstanding. Just the facial reconstructions. This is, of course, just preliminary." The ME still had more to do and would need a day or two before his reports were ready.

"Okay, then. While we wait for more information on them, we can discuss the passenger list, and decide how we will handle our interviews with them. And do you know how soon we will have information on the dead man? I really want to know who he is, if he is really who he said he was."

Passer pulled out his notes on Pinkton, *"No blood on the money as we thought. We didn't find any paperwork on who might have hired him. We just don't know where the money came from. He did have a picture of the two Ruizinho women in his briefcase. I'm really amazed how much these two murdered women looked like them. Even their body shapes were the same. Amazing."* He looked up at Weezie and Karol, who both nodded.

"As to the passenger list, there are 150 passengers on this train, so it will be a very long day of interviewing. We can split it three ways if you would like, so that we each meet with 50 of those passengers. What do you think?"

"There will be 6 less people than that. We have three dead

bodies that would be listed, and then there are my two friends and I. So, 144 people divided by 3 would be 48 each?"

For the first time, the other policeman Karol spoke up. *"Should we make a list of questions so we can be consistent?"*

"Great idea. Let's make that up now." Weezie smiled and reached for her notebook. So did the two policemen.

Then she had another idea. *"I would like to ask my friend Millie to help out with this. She is great at reading people. And she actually is the one who had noticed the two women in the first place, mentioning them to me. She felt that there was something a bit off about them. And, I guess she was right."* The two men nodded. *"That makes us sharing the list 4 ways. So, 36 people for each of us?"* The men nodded again.

"Let me get her to join us before we go into the interview questions. She may have some ideas about that too." And Weezie set off towards her two friends, thinking as she walked, 'What on Earth am I going to say to Bitsy about her not being a part of this?' By the time she got to their table, she had a plan.

"Good morning ladies," she smiled as she sat to join them. *"I have a favor to ask of each of you. Bitsy, would you find a notebook to make notes in and go ask questions of everyone who works on this train? That would be the people in the engine room, the kitchen staff, and all of the stewards. Make sure to get their names and job title and ask them these questions."* She wrote down some questions on her notebook, and tore off the sheet, handing it to Bitsy. *"Now, Bitsy, this will take some finesse, so that you are able to get them to open up and tell you exactly what we need to hear, okay? Do you think you can do that?"*

Bitsy sat straighter in her chair, *"Of course I can. I'll just think of myself as an investigator, like in the movies, and play the part. No problem."* And she rose to begin her work. Weezie smiled to herself, knowing that Bitsy was on a high, being asked to become an actress, something she always said she used to be.

"Millie, the two policemen and I would like you to join us in asking questions of the passengers. We each will meet with 36 people, cutting the passenger list into four separate ones. And we are going to come up with the questions together. Will you come with me and join us at the table?"

Millie simply smiled as if she had been expecting this, and they headed over to the other table.

At the table, when the four were ready, Weezie started the list of questions with *"Let's ask them some questions first about the two women, if they had noticed them, what they saw them do on the train, how they felt when the two women were found murdered. Anything else?"*

The other three seemed to consider this for a moment, and all nodded no. So, she went on.

"I think we need to also ask them about this so-called Detective At Large. Questions such as, did they notice him, did they see him do anything that was unusual, did they see him talk with anyone, and did they see anyone hanging around his cabin or following him. What do you think?"

Millie thought for a moment, and added, *"I think we need to ask everyone if, one, they recognized the two women, and two, if they saw anyone hanging around their cabin, including if they saw the detective doing that."*

"Wonderful, Millie. And if any of you think of anything else we should be asking, please let the others know right away, ok? And what do you think, should we meet everyone in their separate cabins? This might make them feel more comfortable. And when we are done with them, they would be able to leave their cabins to move around the train. Does that sound reasonable?"

"And we each have a fingerprint kit, and we need to get everyone's fingerprints. I should get one to Bitsy too, so she can get ones for the train employees." Weezie was anxious to get

going on this.

Everyone agreed. And so they each took their portion of the passenger list, grabbed their fingerprint kits and headed to their first interviews.

CHAPTER 11

LET'S START INTERVIEWING

"Life is never easy. There is work to be done and obligations to be met – obligations to truth, to justice, and to liberty.."
- John F. Kennedy

With almost 150 passengers on the train, it made for a long day of interviewing.

Millie found that the previous mismatched couple that had caught her interest were on her list. As she met with others, the couple was in the back of her mind. She was anxious to hear what they would have to say. It might be difficult, but she would be sure to just stick to facts, and take a lot of notes, more than with the others, so she wouldn't forget the things she noticed. She was quick to notice the same reaction that she had felt before about them. Something strange was going on with them, as the woman seemed to be looking around their cabin a lot, eyes not focused back at Millie. And the man's eyes remained blank when he tried to talk in broken English.

'Oh,' sighed Millie to herself, thinking about her snap reaction to these people. *'I must be getting quite cranky in my old age. I am too quick to judge people. I know that Weezie is, but with her it was part of her job, like an old habit.'*

While interviewing them, she noticed several more things about them:

-   The woman seemed intense, although she remained quite self-assured.

- The man seemed quite nervous, anxious about something
- They didn't seem to look her in the eye when Millie asked them questions. What were they hiding??
- Their answers told Millie nothing, as they both said they didn't notice anything…about anyone.
- The couple continued to give her a strange feeling.

Millie gave up on the man, telling him he was free to go for now, but kept the woman longer. The woman then looked at Millie, leaned over and whispered to her that she wanted to talk with Weezie, privately. Then she smiled for the first time and said she would wait until Weezie could meet with her.

Millie took a break to go into the dining room for a cup of coffee while she searched for Weezie. As she was returning down the hall, she spotted Weezie, and hurried to her.

"Weezie, I have someone who needs to talk with you, privately she said. On our way to her cabin, let me fill you in on her and her..uh…companion." And she told Weezie what she had felt about them. *"Going purely by appearance, this couple seemed to me to be mismatched. Funny, but they remind me of Boris and Natasha from the Bullwinkle cartoons. I don't want to be so quick to judge people, but these impressions were initially very strong and proved to be even stronger as we talked. The man seemed not just anxious but a bit confused, stuttering a bit as if he were unsure of his words, maybe because he is Russian? And most of the time, he would get a blank look on his face. After just a few minutes, he sat back and hid his face behind a newspaper…very rude to my mind!"*

"Yes, Millie, anything else about the woman?"

" I am thinking she is not who we might think she is. I'm not sure why I say that, but there are secrets hidden behind those dark eyes. And her face barely changed its look, very unfeeling and cold, no matter what my questions were to her."

"Did you learn anything from them?"

"Not a freakin' thing! They barely talked, saying they saw nothing, knew nothing...you know what I mean. And I tried, really I did. But they are made of stone!"

Weezie smiled at Millie, patting her on the shoulder. *"Don't worry, Millie. The truth will come out in the end. We can only do so much at the moment. When we get everyone fingerprinted, we will get a set off to the FBI, who will help us get to the bottom of this."*

When they got to the cabin, Millie walked in first, and introduced the two women. *"Weezie Hightower, I would like you to meet Katherine Ruzinski.."* Katherine nodded. *"Um, her friend Boris Lutoksky has gone on to the dining car. I can get him back if you want."*

Weezie indicated no need. *"Thank you, Millie. I can take it from here."* Weezie remembered seeing this *'couple'* and felt the same. What an odd couple they made. Just like Millie thought, Weezie agreed...exactly like Boris and Natasha. From *'toons'* to tourists?

She reached out her hand to the woman, and sat down opposite her, noting just how dark this woman's eyes were. They looked black, with hardly any white around that dark circle of black. Maybe she wore contacts??

"So, you and Boris are together? Exactly what is your relationship?"

"None of your business." This with a very hard look.

"Could you please share with me how you and Boris met?"

"None of your business."

Weezie sighed, giving the woman one of her intense looks, *"Look Katherine, you wanted to talk with me. Please tell me what you want. I have a lot of other people I need to talk with."*

The woman leaned forward towards Weezie. *"I am a spy. I have been spying on the Ruizinho family for over a year. That is when I met Boris, figuring I could use him to learn more about the inside of their business."* Then she leaned back, with the same look on her face…hard and stonelike.

"How do I know you are telling me the truth?"

"You don't. You will just need to trust me."

"Tell me something only I would know that would convince me that you are indeed a spy. And tell me who you are spying for."

"I can't do that. You will need to put this altogether; I can't do the work for you. Just know that I have secrets. And these secrets need to get to those in the government who will then put that bad man in jail…for his life."

"And who would 'that man' be?"

"You know who I am talking about. I am not Russian, I am Polish. But I was able to mix in with the Russian mob family and learn important things."

"Are you saying that Boris is involved with the Russian mob family?"

"I am telling you nothing at the moment." And she leaned forward again for emphasis. *"But I need you to make sure that nothing happens to me."*

"I will confirm who you are with the people that I know in the government. Meanwhile, make sure you are accessible, I may need to find you quickly." And with that Weezie rose to leave.

When Weezie left the cabin, she wasn't quite sure that this woman was telling the truth. Could she be the '*undercover agent*' that the FBI had placed on the train? Or did this woman just figure out on her own that the FBI would have agents on the train, given the nature of who the murdered women were? Or rather who they were supposed to be. She wished that Bud had given her the identity of their own undercover agent.

As Weezie glanced at her list to see whom she was supposed to interview next, she had trouble shaking a strange feeling about this odd couple. She also reminded herself, *"Millie reads people so well. This particular couple is proving to be very strange indeed, and I am glad that Millie and I can work together to figure them out…or at least try to. Damn, but my brain is tired. I'm getting too old for this.'* And she continued down the corridor to her next interview.

CHAPTER 12

WORKING TOGETHER

"When we do the best we can, we never know what miracle is wrought in our life or the life of another.."
- Helen Keller

That evening, Weezie and the gals met in her cabin. They got Crip on Millie's phone, with Guy in the background on Crip's cell, and they all talked about their days. When it got to Weezie and the gals on the train, there seemed to be quite a bit of confusion on what they had heard, seen and felt.

Millie went first. *"I just don't know what to think. I have met with each of my passengers, and I think quite a few of them are hiding things. I think they may know more than they admit. Why on earth would they want to keep it all secret?"*

Weezie answered her, *"I think there is fear on this train. When two seemingly innocent women are killed, followed by a man, they wonder who might be next. They don't want to say anything, instead they melt into the background. They probably think that if they stand out from the crowd in any way, they may be next. That is understandable, but really makes it hard for us. We all experience being afraid at some time in our lives. We all have that fear 'gene'. Always there...we all need to acknowledge it and deal with it."* And for a moment, she seemed deep in thought.

Guy jumped in, *"What about the staff, Bitsy, did you have any luck with them?"*

Bitsy had a rather blank look on her face at first, then she realized that Guy was talking to her, *"Well, probably they were more open than the passengers. Because they are mostly hidden and no one really sees most of them, I think they were ready to help. It's just that they really WERE hidden and didn't see anything. There was one woman, a female steward, who hinted that she might want to talk with us again. She said, and I wrote it down, 'At the right time, I will come forward with some information. But the time isn't right. When it is, I will be talking with you again. Until then, I have nothing for you."*

Everyone nodded, groaning, as Weezie says, *"Well, that really helps!! Just who is this woman, anyway?"*

Bitsy looked at her notes again, saying as she looked, *"A female steward, with the name, um…oh, here it is, Camilla Ross. She works in our car, along with Steward Madden. But I have never seen her before, have you?"*

Weezie and Millie answered *"No"* at the same time. And a strange look came over Weezie's face. *"Aha, I know now. I really need to talk with our Natasha woman again."* When she got blank looks, she clarified, *"The woman who reminds us of the animated Natasha in Bullwinkle, with the name Katherine. She is supposedly from Poland, but her accent is a bit shaky. She says that she is an undercover agent, but I have my doubts. It doesn't seem to fit, there is something off about her. Not sure what it is. One thing I DO know, is that she seems just too willing to tell me that she is an agent but doesn't mention Bud or even the FBI. And she didn't give any indication of having any ID to prove it. I kept Bud's name out of the conversation, as well as the FBI, as if I had no specific contacts there, and had no inkling that there was an agent on the train. She just didn't use the usual protocol, not even one part of protocol. I think she is lying. Or at least, if she IS an agent, maybe an agent of another organization? She was just so damned unclear."* Weezie was showing her frustration.

Millie added, *"I know what you mean. Both she and her misfit partner just don't add up. Maybe it is because of the*

Bullwinkle cartoons where they are the bad guys."

Everyone laughed. One last question from Guy, *"So, what about the police…did they have any luck with their interviews?"*

Weezie shrugged (as if he could see her through the phone), *"They came up with nothing either."* She paused, *"I think we need to go back to the basics…start all over again."*

That caused a lot of groans, as they all said *"Good night".*

CHAPTER 13

BACK TO THE BASICS

"Keep calm and carry on."
- Winston Churchill

Weezie had trouble sleeping that night. She kept going over everything in her mind. There were just too many unknowns, too many holes. And this '*Natasha*' woman with her comments about being '*undercover*', just didn't add up. And Weezie doesn't like it when things don't add up. So when she went to the dining car for coffee that next morning, she was in the middle of a huge yawn when she heard behind her, *"Good morning Ma'am."* Ah, Policeman Passer.

"Good morning, young man." She closed her mouth before turning around. Yawning in someone's face was rude. But then, she felt another one coming on, and turned back to her coffee and walked to a table as she yawned again.

Passer sat with her, and started off with the business at hand, *"What do you think so far? We really didn't find out anything from anyone. What is our next step?"* His face reflected the concern she was sure he was feeling. Just like her, he needed to get something to hang onto and start a more serious investigation.

"Well," she put her hand on his, *"don't be concerned. We just start over again. You see, people who say things in their first interview, especially if they are covering something up, might slip up when interviewed again. It is much easier to recall the truth than any fiction they may have invented."* And she smiled at him.

As they both sipped their coffee, they enjoyed the quiet, since they were up so early. Only one other table had someone sitting there, people that Weezie didn't recognize. She thought, *'They must have been on someone else's list.'*

Passer looked at her, feeling unsure about just exactly what she meant about truth and fiction. *"If they are hiding something, how do we get them to open up?"*

"Actually, it isn't that hard. We simply interview them again, asking the same questions, giving them a chance to add something to their original comments. We simply tell them that sometimes in times like this, people remember events that in the first 24 hours may be blocked. Memories are like that. When someone senses danger, it tends to distract them from remembering exactly what they may have seen…something like that. It gives them a chance to rethink things. And it is not like we are accusing them, just simply asking for their help by remembering something…any little thing. Passer, do you understand?"

"Ah, yes, I do. Brilliant!"

"Okay, let's start over again, same lists for the same interviewers. This time, we try to dig a little deeper."

With this, they set off to fill in Millie and Policeman Weiss on the plan.

The first half of that day was filled with once again keeping everyone in their cabins and going over the statements given the day before. Some of the people they talked to did remember something else to add to their *'testimony'* but overall didn't help that much more…disappointing the four interviewers.

When they reconvened in the dining car to review notes together, Passer, Weiss, Millie and Weezie didn't look very hopeful.

"Well, we did try. I don't see anything new that actually will help us solve this thing," said Weezie. She looked as tired as she felt, reaching for a large mug of coffee.

Millie leaned towards Weezie, *"You decided to do the followup interview with Boris and Natasha, er, I mean Katherine. What do you think about them now?"*

"I am disappointed about that too. I think Natasha/Katherine is inferring something that is not true. I think she is indeed 'undercover', but not for us nor the FBI. I found out something about her when I called Bud a little while ago."

"Oh?" asked Passer, as the three leaned in together to hear what Weezie had to say.

"The FBI received the fingerprint package we sent and they have started working on them. Bud actually did a little digging into who this woman really is. And he answered the questions we have about her. No, she is not working with us. She is not the agent on the train. I wish I had talked with him before I did the second interview with her. But now, I am ready for another serious talk with her. And without Boris, because I don't think she wants him to know who she really is."

"Well, who is she??" Millie asked.

Weezie looked at her watch. *"Let's meet back here in an hour. I will fill you in then. I am going to talk with her again."* And she rose and walked away, leaving the three a bit frustrated. They didn't appreciate being kept in the dark on this. At least they would learn more in an hour's time. Now, more coffee, with something to eat to pass the time.

CHAPTER 14

WHAT'S GOING ON??

"Life would be tragic if it weren't funny."
- Stephen Hawking

Weezie knocked on the cabin door, and Katherine/Natasha opened the door with a frown on her face. *"What is your problem? Why do you need to see me again? Did you forget something?"* She seemed very irritated. Weezie felt that perhaps there was some fear mixed in with that. Maybe fear of having her real identity discovered?

"Yes, I did forget one thing, Katherine. Let's sit down so we can talk," and Weezie moved to sit opposite where Katherine usually sat.

Weezie first took a long hard look at this woman, who was not who she claimed.

"Well??" the woman asked, more irritated than before.

"I don't mean to make you anxious Katherine...or should I say Oksmiella?" Katherine/Oksmiella's face turned a very pale shade of white.

"I don't understand."

"Yes you do. I know who you are, and why you have been spying on the Ruizinho organization. I know about how your sister had gotten mixed up with them, and that she was killed because she wanted to get out. But there is no getting out of that kind of organization, unless it is through death. Isn't that right?"

Katherine/Oksmiella hung her head, beginning to shake with tears ready to fall. *"She was my sister...my sister! How could they do that to such an amazing, beautiful person? They all deserve to die!"* With that, she stood up, color now from white to red, looking very flushed and angry.

"Sit down. We need to talk about this."

She stood stubborn and proud, then her body seemed to crumble as it fell back to her seat. *"No, no, I should be the one to die, not her!"* And the tears increased, while she covered her face with hands that shook.

"Listen to me. We will make sure you are safe. We will protect you. We will want you to testify against the organization."

"And be killed like those two women? HE killed them, you know. Boris did!"

"I'm not sure he was the one who killed them."

"But he was supposed to. That is why we were to be on this train. To kill the two Ruizinho women so they wouldn't be able to testify. I will be next if I agree to testify." And her face took on a stubborn, fierce look.

'*So this woman didn't know that the two women were not the actual Ruizinhos,'* Weezie realized. Then she wondered if she should tell her. No, it was not her job to do that. The FBI agents should tell her when they felt it was the right time. She just needed to convince her to keep quiet and keep her safe. Weezie realized that she hadn't asked Passer where exactly he had taken Boris. They needed to keep him away from everyone after Millie had interviewed him again. But she was positive of what she was going to say next.

"Boris didn't kill the two women. I have had him detained, away from you. But he didn't do it. Perhaps he was with you to kill you?"

"No, Boris wouldn't kill me. He loves me. He was the way I got into the organization. I am using him to get to them."

There was a knock at the door. Both women stopped and stared at one another. "Who is it?" asked Katherine/Oksmiella.

"I am looking for Weezie," came the answer. But Weezie didn't recognize the woman's voice. She rose to answer the door, ready for anything.

It was a woman dressed in a steward outfit. She looked at Weezie, "I need to talk with you out here in the hallway." And she took Weezie's hand, pulling her out the door. As Weezie pulled the door shut behind her, the woman took out an official FBI badge and explained. "I am Camilla. I was told to find you and tell you who I am. The FBI are on their way, almost here. About 15 minutes out, and I am supposed to stay with you until they get here."

'Aha, this would be the undercover FBI agent,' Weezie thought. "I understand. I am going to ask you for your help. The woman inside this cabin is a witness against the Ruizinho organization. We need to keep her safe. I would like you to stay with her. Don't let her out of this cabin, and don't let anyone in. I will come to get you both when it is time. Did Bud, rather Executive Director Walsh explain that I am in charge here?" The woman nodded. "Then, please stay with this woman, keep her safe. I will be back after the FBI arrive, OK?"

Agent/Steward Camilla nodded, and entered the cabin, closing and locking it behind her.

Weezie headed back to the dining car, to let everyone know that the FBI would be here soon. She had just enough time to sit, eat a couple bites of a sandwich, a few sips of coffee, when she heard the helicopter. Then the four of them headed to meet the agents. The other three still wanted to know the truth about the Polish woman, and were trying to be patient until Weezie could fill them in.

CHAPTER 15

MEDICAL EXAMINER

"Never take life seriously. Nobody gets out alive anyway."
- Anonymous

The FBI agents jumped out of the helicopter and headed straight towards Weezie and her group. There was a smile on the face of one of them, someone that she hadn't seen in a few years. She smiled back at him, stepping forward.

"Well, well, Agent Willis, how long has it been?" She reached for his hand, grasping it in both of hers. She remembered him well and was glad he was there.

"Ah, Weezie, you haven't changed a bit. Still got that sassy gal look," and he leaned forward to kiss her cheek. Everyone stood around, looking a bit confused.

Willis stepped back, laughed, saying, *"So, our Executive Director wants us to help you out here. You know I would follow you anywhere."* Another laugh, with Weezie joining in.

Weezie turned back to her group, *"This is Special Agent Willis, someone whom I have enjoyed working with before, and a darned good agent."* And she turned back to Willis, *"And I would like to introduce you to the town Police, Mr. Passer and Mr. Weiss, and this is one of my gals Millie."*

"Ah, one of the Cackle Gang, I have heard about. Weezie, I was so sorry to hear about your husband Earl's passing," and gave her a hug. *"Millie, glad to meet you."* Then he pointed to his agent partner, *"And everyone, this is Special Agent Mather. I*

believe he has a file for you, Weezie. Agent…" And Mather handed the file to her.

Weezie nodded, "Thanks for this. Why don't we all collect in the dining car and make a plan for our next step." And they followed her, no questions asked.

Weezie asked both policemen and Millie to talk about the people they had interviewed. Then Weezie added from her own notes. She noticed Millie looking at her expectantly, probably about more information on the 'Natasha' woman. But Weezie said, "There is more about one of the passengers, Katherine from Poland. I will fill you in on her later. First, I need to find out about Boris. Passer, he is safely parked in one of your jail cells, right?" She looked at Passer who nodded.

"Why is he in jail, Weezie? What did he do?" asked Millie.

"He actually had a part in all of this, but he did not kill the two women. I have a theory about that, but we need to talk with the Medical Examiner first. Then I will fill you all in."

There was a lot to think about. They took a moment to sit back in their chairs, sip some coffee and consider everything that had happened. Weezie gave them about five minutes to do that.

Agent Willis spoke first, "I think it is time to meet with the Medical Examiner. We have three bodies to take a close look at." He pointed to the file Weezie still held. "And there is something in there that we will discuss after we see the two women at the morgue."

It didn't take long to get to the Medical Examiner's office, in the basement of the tallest building in this small town, where the police offices occupied the top floor, the fifth one. Small towns, ah yes, once again, you gotta love them.

The Medical Examiner was busy working on Detective At Large Harold W. Pinkton's body when they arrived. He looked up at them, nodded at Passer and Weiss, covered the body, and went to the sink to wash up. Then he shook hands with everyone. *"Good to meet you, I am Doctor Bookman. I have much to share with you about these bodies. Why don't we start with the two women,"* and walked ahead of them over to where the two women were stored in a cold storage cabinet. As the ME began to pull out the two drawers with the bodies, Weezie felt shivers go up and down her spine, and looking over at Millie saw that she too was feeling the same. They stared at one another for a moment, then Weezie stepped forward to take a look at the younger of the two women.

"Can you tell us about this one first, Dr. Bookman?"

"Well, this poor young thing was only about 17 I would say, previously in good health. She had a facial reconstruction done of her nose and jaw area. Her eyes and mouth were still hers, except she wore colored contact lenses. I guess she was pretending to be someone else?"

Weezie nodded. *"Anything else you can tell us about her?"*

"No, not really. Just an innocent young thing. What a shame."

"And her injuries?"

"Oh, yes, of course. Sorry. I have a daughter the same age. Just threw me off for a minute." He cleared his throat, *"She was stabbed once in the heart, an injury which killed her immediately. Then, for some reason, the killer slit her throat, almost as an afterthought."* He made a stern face, *"Monster...who would do such a thing?"*

"We will find out soon," replied Weezie. *"Then, what can you tell us about the older woman?"*

"She was early 40s, once again in good health, well before anyway. She looked like she had given birth at some point,

judging by her uterus. Also her hips were a little widened as a result of a pregnancy. She had the same exact death, instantaneous with the stab wound in the heart, with the throat being slit afterwards. Damn injuries on an otherwise health woman."

"And she had a facial reconstruction done too?" asked Agent Willis.

"Yes, she did. Interesting though…this was her second facial reconstruction. Her previous one, old scar tissue, showed that her ears were 'clipped', as well as a nose job. The latest one showed her eyes had been widened a bit and her mouth changed, made wider with fuller lips. And her hair was dyed recently."

Agent Willis nodded to the file in Weezie's hands, so she took a quick look. There was a picture of a woman in her 40s, probably of what she looked like before, with some notes on her previous surgery, as well as her most recent reconstruction. She looked up at Willis with a puzzled look.

Agent Willis asked the Doctor, *"Did you find anything strange near their heads, Doctor?"*

The Doctor stared back at the Agent, then it hit him, *"Oh, yes. Both of these women had a very small metal object that had been inserted in the back of their upper necks, just below where the brain stem is. See here in the back of her head."* He indicated a spot that he had sewn back together. Then he reached for a plastic container, *"Here is the one I found in her neck. And this other one holds the young woman's that I also found. Do you know what they are?"*

Willis nodded, *"Yes. They are tracking devices. We put them there, just near the hair line so it would have been hidden. We needed to know exactly where these women were at all times."*

"I can read the file later on. That will help me put the info

together on these two women. Now, what about the man?" asked Weezie, pointing to the table where Pinkton lay.

"Yes," said Doctor Bookman, "I had just completed my autopsy on him when you came in. Let's move over to his body and I can show you."

With one last look at the two women, the Doctor covered them, pushed the drawers back into the cold storage wall unit, and moved to the examination table in the middle of the room.

"This man was in his early 60s, very overweight, quite lax about cleanliness, and his organs showed that he just didn't take very good care of himself. It looked like his kidneys would stop working within the next couple of years. His liver showed that he had been a heavy drinker and it too would only last a couple of years more. His stomach showed signs of recent ulceration, probably from his drinking and eating the wrong food. His body was in bad shape for a man who was still young. He must have done a lot of walking, as he had flat feet, fallen arches. And…"

"Doctor, how did he die?" Passer was losing patience.

"He was stabbed in the heart. Now, interesting that it is in a different place than the two women. With the man, the knife was angled upward, deeper on the right side, and into the right atria, whereas the two women had been stabbed in a straight path into their lower chambers, specifically, the left ventricle."

"And what do you gather from that, Doctor?" asked Agent Willis.

"What I believe happened, is that we have two different killers here. The women's killer was about the same height or a little taller than them, plunging the knife straight ahead. But the throats being slashed were deeper on the left side. This means their killer was right-handed. The man's killer was a bit shorter than he was, because of the upward angle. Also, that person was left-handed and strong. The victim was fat and not in good shape, but still fairly strong. So, perhaps a short left-handed man?" The Doctor stood back, crossing his arms, waiting for their reactions and questions.

"Exactly what type of doctor are you?" asked Millie.

"I am a General Practitioner and have been for over 25 years. And I have lived and served this town for 20 years. Also, my wife is an attorney up on the third floor of this building. We married, then settled here together."

The two policemen looked at one another, smiling at the memory of their meeting her on the elevator a couple of days ago. 'Pre-train' thought Weiss.

Weezie gave them a stern look, since smiling in a morgue would be considered quite rude. They got it, and both wiped the smiles off their faces.

"Can you tell us, Doctor, what the exact height of all three murder victims were?" asked Weezie, ready to add to her notes she had been taking since they arrived in the morgue.

"The younger woman was approximately 5'3" and the older woman was 5'5. This man was about 5'8" tall."

"Hmm," Weezie responded. She looked lost in thought for a moment, then smiled and thanked the Doctor for his time, and they all shook hands again and left.

CHAPTER 16

FINALLY A NAME

"Every strike brings me closer to the next home run."
- Babe Ruth

There was much to discuss for this crime solving group of six, yet many more questions. They returned to the dining car, taking a table separated from other passengers for privacy. At first, they sat in silence, each one rethinking what had happened so far in this case.

Then Weezie leaned forward and quietly said, *"Does anyone want to start with their thoughts? I think we have quite a few answers, but it seems there are even more questions. We DO know that we have two different killers here. The murdered women tell us that their killer was between 5'5" and perhaps 5'8" and right-handed. Pinkton's killer was shorter than 5'8" and left-handed. It's always amazing to me how a dead person's body can basically 'talk to us'."* Everyone nodded.

"What do you think, Millie?" She looked over at her friend.

Millie sat for a moment silently mulling things over, then started. *"I think we still have a lot of questions, such as does it matter who these two women really were? I mean, their exact identity?"*

FBI agent Mather answered her question, *"We do know who they are...were. They were mother and daughter. Susan Brown has worked with us before, as you learned by the fact that this was her second facial reconstruction. She is...was a single* mother and was paid well for that job. So, this time, she received double the pay to bring in her daughter Meredith. All of this was planned months ago, actually almost a year ago. We have been working on the Ruizinho crime family for many years. And when the mother and daughter came forward to testify, we were able to pull in the Browns to work with us. Dangerous work, but they needed the money, and were willing to sign all the waivers, even a will in case something happened. Which it did." He hung his head for a moment.

They all felt it, sadness that these two women died doing a job for the government.

"But, please keep in mind that they didn't do the job for the good of our country, they simply needed the money. And Susan knew the ropes…so to speak. There are photos of them before the surgery in the file we gave Weezie."

They were curious, so Weezie pulled out the photos to look at. And she commented, "It is actually quite amazing to see the transformation in both of these women. And the fact that the mother Susan had it done twice. Maybe that's why Millie had noticed how stiff her facial expressions were."

"Yes, I noticed it right away. And of course, the first thing I thought of was - Botox injections? You know how they can sometimes freeze your face." Millie looked at the others. "I just happened to notice them, mainly for that, I think. Strange, huh? Little did I know what was really going on. But it didn't take Weezie long before she recognized them. Rather who they were meant to look like."

"Hmmm, I wonder," said Weezie. They all looked at her. "I think I need to read this file. Then, Agents, I may want to talk with you more. Please stay and talk or eat. I'll be in my cabin and will join you when I finish the file." With that, she got up and left.

Millie stared at her back, "What is she up to now?"

CHAPTER 17

ARE THEY CONNECTED??

*"Do not dwell in the past, do not dream of the future,
concentrate the mind on the present moment."*
- Buddha

As Weezie read through the file, she learned that the previous case that Susan Brown had worked on with the FBI was for a case involving another crime family, but a smaller organization. The current case, the Ruizinho organization was one of the largest in the country. But she wondered if there were some sort of connection between the two cases. Could someone have been watching Susan due to the previous case, seeing her and her daughter involved in this case, then took this opportunity to kill them?

Her head began to hurt. '*Coffee, I need more coffee,*' she thought as she grabbed the file, returning to the dining car.

Everyone was still there at the table, heads together, discussing ideas. When Weezie, coffee mug in hand, joined them, at first they didn't look up. Mather was talking in hushed tones to the others, *"Millie, that is a good theory, but I'm not sure that the two cases Susan worked on are connected. But we can look into it."*

When they heard Weezie's quiet chuckle, he looked at her, *"What?"*

"Millie, my friend, great minds think alike. I was just coming back to discuss this same thought. Mather, since the two cases Susan helped you with were both crime families, could they be connected? Could someone from the smaller organization want to

somehow break up the larger one by killing these two? Have there been any occasions where these two organizations were connected in any way? Did they ever work together before?"

FBI Agent Mather was quiet for a moment. "*Weezie, what did you say this Polish Natasha person's name was?*"

Millie answered him, "*Her name is Katherine Ruzinski.*"

"*Actually, Millie, I think he means her real name. That was Oksmiella, same last name, Ruzinski. She got involved, she said, because someone from the Russian organization caused the death of her sister.*"

Mather sat back, crossed his arms, the muscles in his cheeks working for a moment, then leaned back in, "*That is it! A Polish woman, same last name, was killed along with her Russian crime family boyfriend, a couple of years back. But that wasn't the Ruizinho family, it was the other one. Why is she so interested in this case? It doesn't make sense.*"

"*Then let's ask her. Mather, you come with me,*" and Weezie stood up with a determined look on her face. "*We need to find out what is in this woman's mind. We need answers.*"

Millie watched them walk away and wondered just how much more confusing this murder investigation could get.

CHAPTER 18

TWO FACES

"The minute that you're not learning I believe you're dead."
- Jack Nicholson

Weezie and Mather saw a very angry woman waiting for them in her cabin. *"Where is Boris? I demand to see him! I have questions for him!"* Oksmiella was so angry that her face was beet red, and her eyes were flashing so much that they looked as if they may jump right out of her head.

"Oksmiella, please sit down, we need to talk," answered Weezie to her.

"NO! NO! I will not talk until I see Boris!"

"Why do you need to see Boris? You, yourself told me that he had murdered the two women, remember?" asked Weezie.

"I may have been mistaken about that. I was so angry with him. Sometimes he is just so stupid. I need to see him! NOW!"

Mather stepped between the two women, *"I think that can be arranged. Come with us."* And he turned around, opened the cabin door slowly, giving her time to think about it.

She and Weezie followed him out. *"Where is he? Where are you keeping him?"*

"You will see in just a few minutes." He led them towards the dining car, where he waved at Policeman Posser to join them. Then the four of them headed off the train.

Weezie knew to trust Agent Mather, but she still wondered what he had in mind. She would find out in just a few minutes.

When they got to the five-story building and headed up in the elevator, Weezie looked over at Oksmiella. Her rigid face was hard to read, but Weezie sensed some fear mixed in with the anger. *'Maybe she thinks she will be taken to jail too? She probably figured out that Boris was already taken there.'* Weezie felt that old excitement that she used to when working on cases. That sense of wonderment and excitement, not knowing what the next minute would bring. Her headache was gone.

You couldn't see Boris when you entered the police jail, as he was being kept in the last cell. Instead of heading there, Mather reached over to the first cell (all the cells were empty), leading the two women in, then nodding at Passer, who closed the door behind them, waiting just outside the cell. The local policeman was wondering what was going to happen too. You could see it in his face…confusion plus excitement. He was probably thinking, *'Oh, this is going to be good.'*

"Oksmiella, please sit down," Mather said as he showed Weezie to the opposite bunk, sitting beside her.

"What is this?! I demand to see Boris! Why am I in a cell?"

Suddenly another voice joined them from afar, *"Katie, girl, is that you? My Katie?"* It was Boris. Weezie smiled, understanding the plan.

"Boris? Boris? Where are you?" she yelled, standing up.

"I am here, in a cell. Find me," he answered.

"I need to see him…ALONE!" Oksmiella's face was red again.

"I don't think so," responded Mather. *"We need some answers from you first."*

She sat back down, leaning towards him, *"No,"* she whispered, *"He can't hear my words. He must not know who I really am. I am still undercover. Please…"*

"Okay, then, let's go somewhere more private," Mather nodded to Passer, and led them out of the cell, with Passer in the lead.

You could see the slight knowing smile on Passer's face. *'Yup, this is really going to get interesting,'* he was thinking.

CHAPTER 19

AN ANSWER...OR NOT?

"Life shrinks or expands in proportion to one's courage."
- Anais Nin

Once again, Oksmiella's face had turned from red to pale and worried. This was the face that Weezie preferred. But, she wondered, '*Are we going to get any truthful answers from this woman who seems so intent on protecting herself?*' She could only hope. Because if not, she had no idea if any of them had a Plan B.

The room was specifically for interrogations, with a huge mirror on one wall...of course, so that anyone on the other side of it could watch. '*Yup, just like in the movies,*' thought Millie, who had arrived with Weiss and was selected to stay with Weezie and Mather in the room. Willis and the two local policemen were stationed in the next room, on the other side of the two-way mirror.

Even though Oksmiella looked pale and worried, she managed to sit straight in the chair, offering a far-away look in her dark eyes. Still Weezie had hope as she began, *"Oksmiella, let's talk about your sister."*

This broke through her protective wall. Those dark eyes began to flash, then tear up. *"Why must we talk about her? Let her go, she is dead."*

"I know that, but she is the one you want to avenge. We would really like to know more about her. Was she younger?" Weezie already knew the answer, but it was a good place to

begin.

"Yes, she was my baby sister. We were close," as Oksmiella's face began to look downward and her shoulders began to lower. She looked back up at Weezie, *"She was SO beautiful, smart and,"* a little laugh, *"even a bit sassy. She was so very clever. Then, HE came into her life."*

"Who was he?" asked Weezie.

"His name was Maxim Volkov. He worked for the large Russian syndicate in this country."

"Tell us what happened to them?"

"They both died. Adilajda was so in love with Maxim, she wrote me these letters about him. She wrote me that he had so much money, that they did many things, went many places. I began to suspect all was not right, because she said that he worked for an organization, but it was not a 9-5 job. He was more 'on-call' instead. It just didn't sound right."

Weezie leaned in a bit towards her, *"What did you do?"*

"I made arrangements to come to this country and find her, try to find out more about this young man, and help her. I had such a bad feeling about it all." Then tears began to flow. *"But I was too late. This was over a year ago, and it still hurts so much."*

"Yes, I understand. I am so sorry. It must have been so hard for you."

"It was HELL!!" She stood up, face bright red, almost purple. *"And you people,"* pointing to the FBI agent, *"you were no help! I went to your office in New York City and wanted to talk with someone to find out how I could find these monsters who killed my sister and her boyfriend. But no one told me anything! No one helped me!"*

Weezie patiently looked at her, pointing to her chair,

"Please, Oksmiella, sit down. Now we are ready to help you."

"Sure you are!! Too late! I want to get out of here! I don't like prisons. My father was in a prison for many years, dying in one. I need to leave here!" And she made for the door.

Millie rose and went to her, taking this distraught woman into her arms, *"Oh, honey, I am so sorry. We all are. We really DO want to help you. And I am so sorry we couldn't save your sister. But we can save YOU, please let us."*

The tall woman looked down at this older lady, who had such soft eyes and a concerned look on her face and began to cry. Millie helped her to the table and sat beside her, holding her hand. Millie talked to her softly, *"Take your time. We will listen to everything you have to say. Take a deep breath."*

Weezie was watching her friend handle this woman, thinking to herself, *'Millie is just that kind of person…a fixer of broken things. And she does it so well.'*

After a deep breath, then another, Oksmiella was ready, *"Yes, I got no help. I had to find out as much as I could on my own. I found out that the Russian organization was under Akim Ruizinho. A little over a year ago, I met Boris who works for him, and began to learn as much as I could. I thought I could somehow get to Ruizinho and avenge my sister. I really didn't care about Maxim, just Adilajda. She deserved for me to 'kill her killers'."*

There was a look on Agent Mather's face that Weezie was trying to read and NEEDED to read. What was she missing??

She turned her attention back to Oksmiella, *"What happened then? What did you do to get closer to the organization and find out your answers?"*

"It was SO hard to get information. I had to begin a relationship with Boris," she smiled, *"what a little fat stooge. It was so easy to get his attention, then begin to pull information from*

him. But it took time. He may not be the brightest, but he is very protective of 'the family'. On this train, we were headed back to New York where he was going to actually introduce me to Ruizinho. Because of his wife and daughter being witnesses against him, his organization has become quite tight and protective of him. That's why it took me so long, working on Boris. They have brain washed him so well, but," with a smile, *"I have gotten through to him now. He adores me, would do anything for me."* Then she stood up, *"I need to see Boris, NOW!"*

Millie looked at Weezie, then stood beside the woman, *"Yes, I understand, and you will see him. But we have one more question for you. Could you sit back down for just a minute?"*

They sat, with Oksmiella glaring at everyone.

Agent Mather took a deep breath, paused, then decided to share some information with Oksmiella. *"I am so sorry for your loss. We should have helped you. If we had, then you wouldn't have wasted your time this past year."*

She looked at him, eyes glaring, *"What do you mean, waste my time? My time wasn't wasted, I had to be very careful that they wouldn't find out she was my sister."*

"They wouldn't have known anything about her, nor about Maxim." He paused, then continued, *"Oksmiella, you have been going after the wrong organization."*

She stood and shouted, *"WHAT?! What are you saying?"*

Millie looked up at her thinking *'Wow, she certainly has an explosive personality.'*

"Please sit down, and I will explain," Mather pointed to her chair. Millie reached up for Oksmiella's hand, slowly pulling her down to the chair. *"There are two main organizations of Russian gangsters in this country. The largest is the Ruizinho crime organization. And the second large one is the Sidorov*

76

organization."

"Who is that? I didn't find anything about them in my research," Oksmiella responded, quietly. She appeared to be scared of learning more.

"That is the organization that Maxim Volkov was a member of. That is the one that he pulled your sister into, to work for them. That is the organization that killed both Maxim and Adilajda. Not the Ruizinho family."

"NO! NO! NO!" Oksmiella began to pound on the table, huge tears falling from those dark eyes. She was visibly falling apart. Her head fell onto her arms, crossed on the table.

Weezie looked over at Millie, then at Mather, wondering what was next?

Then Mather spoke, *"Oksmiella. We are going to help you get to the Sidorov organization and their leader Dimitriy Sidorov. You have proven to be an amazing 'under cover' spy, and we could use you on our team. What do you say?"*

She looked up, totally broken and slumping over in her chair. She would need time to handle this, *"I don't know. I just don't know. I am so tired of all of this."*

"You still want to avenge your sister?"

She took several moments to simply breathe, then *"Yes."*

Now Weezie understood that look on Mather's face. *'Can you imagine for the past year, trying to break into that organization just to find out that it was the wrong one?'* thought Weezie. She also took a deep breath, then to Mather, *"What about Boris? What do we do about him?"*

With this question, Oksmiella lifted her head back up, *"I don't want to see that man ever again. I used him, let him fall in love with me. But I am done with him and his wrong organization. I don't care about him. Do what you want to with him."*

Mather, Millie and Weezie looked at one another, wondering, *'Now what??'*

CHAPTER 20

A NEW IDEA

"When we strive to become better than we are, everything around us becomes better too."
- Paulo Coelho

Weezie figured that Oksmiella was no longer useful in their case against the Ruizinho family, and felt that if she were forced to see Boris again, that poor lump of a man would fall apart. Yet he probably would have enough sense to know what she had done. The woman's face was no longer a mask to her emotions. She had fallen apart and needed time to pull herself back together. So, he talked with Willis who decided to take her back to FBI headquarters, where they could pull her into their investigation against the Sidorov organization.

They had decided to let Boris sit in jail for another day, leaving him to wonder what was going to happen. They hoped that he would be ready to be interrogated the next day.

As Mather, Millie, Weezie and Passer returned to the dining car for another meeting, Weezie began to feel as if she were missing something. There was so much going on in this case, so many clues, so many questions with only a few answers so far, she was beginning to get a headache again. She needed some food. They decided to eat dinner, each with their own thoughts, before discussing the case again.

Weezie loved to have coffee with all of her meals. Some people get too much caffeine from that, but not her. Her brain seemed to need it, just as her body needed food. It also helped to take away her headache.

As they all sat around the table, full tummies being filled to the brim with wonderful deserts, Weezie began the conversation. *"Well, that was quite interesting. Agent Mather, now that we know Oksmiella was going after the wrong Russian organization, what should we do with Boris?"* Then looking around the table, *"Do any of you think he is involved with the three murders?"*

Millie was the one to speak up first, *"Yes, I do. He is a seedy little man, always disappearing who knows where, and I don't trust one hair on his head...so to speak."* She actually looked quite angry. Then looked over at Mather, *"How could you let her go after the wrong Russian organization? That was really cruel!"*

He actually smiled as he looked back at her, *"We knew all about her sister and boyfriend's deaths, and we have been trying to find a way to get into the Sidorov family since then. If we could use their deaths to at least get to Dmitriy, we would have more luck breaking up that organization too, just like we are doing with the Ruizinho organization. Now we have Oksmiella to do that. I think we will make progress more quickly on that case. She will be a valuable asset to us."* He seemed pleased with himself.

Weezie could feel the anger bringing color to her face, *"Damn, Mather! I agree with what Millie has said. The FBI has been cruel to her! Why didn't you pull her in, explain earlier that she was going after the wrong organization and begin helping her way before now?"*

Mather sighed, looked down at the table for a moment, then answered, *"We are after Boris."* Then he excused himself from the table and left.

'Wait...what??' thought both Millie and Weezie.

CHAPTER 21

SOCIAL MEDIA??

"Life's tough, but it's tougher when you're stupid."
- John Wayne

That night, almost too tired to talk but missing the other gals, Weezie asked Millie and Bitsy to come to her cabin for a call to Guy and Crip.

After learning how Crip was doing health wise, which was a lot of joking around but no real information, Weezie gave up on asking more about her wellbeing. So, she began filling them in the very long day that she and Millie had.

"Wow, that's all pretty crazy," comment Crip. *"So, the FBI is after Boris? I thought he was a bit on the stupid side. Figures. You think you know someone…"*

"Crip, I feel like I have been missing something, but I just can't put my finger on it. My brain is overworked, and I am really feeling it. I hardly remember my name tonight."

Crip laughed, *"You are Louise 'Weezie' Hightower, a fantastic crime fighter and solver, and great friend to me, Millie and Bitsy."* A pause, *"And Guy Davis, who is standing right here. Sit down man, take a load off."*

They could hear Guy laughing in the background. *"Hi, Guy, how are you?"* Asked Bitsy. Then she giggled. Weezie groaned.

"Doing just fine. As you know, Crip has an amazing sense

of humor. I laugh all the time, hanging out with her."

"Oh, my God!! I can't believe I did that!" shouted Weezie.

"What?" the rest of them asked.

"Detective At Large Pitkin. Oh, my God, I forgot all about it! I am such a duncehead, a fool..."

Millie reached over and put her hand on Weezie's, *"What are you talking about, my dear?"*

Weezie hung her head as if she were being whipped, *"His logbook!! I forgot all about it! There has to be something that will help us more in there. How could I forget all about it?"* She stood, began to look through her things, *"Now, where did I put it?"*

Bitsy, as usual, was in the dark, *"What on Earth are you talking about?"*

Weezie turned around. *"Okay, everyone. Remember when we found Pitkin's body?"* Nods all around...even Crip and Guy were nodding, unseen. *"I took his logbook, thinking I should read it and see what he had in it. I bet it will tell us who hired him, and maybe what he was really doing following the two women around. I just can't believe I forgot all about it!"* And she continued looking around her cabin.

Guy jumped into the conversation, *"Weezie, sit down. You can look for it after our call. Take a deep breath. Sit down!"*

Weezie stopped, looked down at the talking cell phone, and sat down. *"Okay."*

Guy continued, *"So you said you know the real names of the two women victims, a mother and daughter. The daughter was a teenager. I bet she was on social media. How about I take a look and see what I can find there? I feel like I am not helping you at all. What do you think? It will make me feel better, helping a little..."*

"Oh, Guy, what a wonderful idea," sighed Weezie. *"I do need your help and you are so great at doing that kind of thing. Yes, please. The names are Susan and Meredith Brown. Meredith is the daughter. I will have Millie text you a picture of what she really looked like."* Weezie's cell didn't work very well in her cabin.

"A picture would help find her. Thanks. I will have something for you by tomorrow. Too late tonight. I will need a clear head. I'm not as young as I used to be." A giggle from Bitsy.

"Guy, if you find out anything at all before tomorrow night, will you text me and we will set an earlier time to talk about it? I don't want to wait if you do find out something important. Okay?" Weezie sounded relieved.

"Okay. And I can't wait to find something…anything," he said. And they all said, *"Good night".*

CHAPTER 22

FINGER PRINT CONFIRMATION

"You only pass through this life once, you don't come back for an encore."
- Elvis Presley

Weezie had met with Millie, Bitsy and the two FBI agents Willis (had returned from taking Oksmiella to FBI headquarters) and Mather for breakfast. She had been so exhausted the night before that she finally enjoyed a good night's sleep. She was feeling better about the logbook too, as she was planning to go back to her cabin to dig into it.

She said her goodbyes at the table, where they had set a time to meet up later after she had gathered information from Pinkton's notes. As she was heading down the corridor to her cabin, her phone rang. Since she doesn't get very good reception on the train, it made a sad little twitter sound, but it was definitely an incoming call. She saw FBI Director Bud Walsh's name pop up so she headed into the train's public bathroom. That is where she got the best reception for her particular phone. For their nightly calls back home, they had been using Millie's larger, newer model made by a different company with a different server. For some reason Millie's service had proven to be stronger.

"Hey, Weezie, how's it going over there? I have heard reports from Willis and Mather, but felt I needed to check in with you."

She paused a moment before responding, *"It's going better*

since I remembered a potentially important piece of the puzzle, Detective At Large Pinkton's logbook. I am headed back to my cabin to jump into it, with the hopes that some answers may be in there."

"Good thinking. Let me know what you find. You can text me anytime, you know. It seems like I live on my phone, just like everyone else in the world." Then he laughed, *"Sometimes I'm holding my cell in one hand while I talk on my office phone with the other. I lead a crazy life."*

Weezie laughed with him, *"I can actually picture that. It would look good as a cartoon in the newspaper."*

"Yup, that's me, a toon. Hey, speaking of which, we are going to talk with the cartoon character Natasha, rather in real live Oksmiella, later today. Last night, she arrived by helicopter. Willis dropped her off and couldn't wait to get to you all out there…in the middle of nowhere. How do you like it out there…'somewhere' in the Southwest?"

"I don't really know. I hardly have time to brush my teeth, let alone look around our host town, even though it is smaller than just about any town I have ever been in. I'm sure there is some charm here, but I haven't had much free time to search for it."

More laughter from both of them.

Weezie had a thought about Bahrump Junction that she shared with him, *"One thing I have noticed here is that everyone I have met knows everyone else, and most are related to one another. It's like this town once started somewhere between an idea and a place. I'm sure it took generations before the idea and place became inseparable. Why leave? You can escape a town, but you can't escape blood. Everyone seems happy to be living here together. A good example of that is these two young policemen, Passer and Weiss, first cousins, and the elder Passer, father/uncle, who is Chief of Police. It's all very neatly wrapped up, like a package…one town, one big family. Well, with just a few exceptions."* She paused for a moment.

"I have a question for you, Bud, 'Why are you so interested in Boris?"

"Sorry, Weezie" he paused, *"You will need to wait for our answer to that question for a little while more. We are doing something that will prove our theory…or not. Then you will know about it."*

"Is he someone special?"

"Possibly. Probably."

"Okay, guess I'll need to wait. Do you have anything you CAN tell me about?"

"Oh, yeah, fingerprints. Some interesting things turned up, not to help the case that much, but just interesting. Firstly, we made sure our two female victims were the Browns. And they are. And now we know who Natasha/Katherine/Oksmiella is. Most of the other passengers and personnel are who they say they are. And of course, you met our undercover agent. She has actually returned here too, no more need for her to stay on the train. I think we have everything quite figured out, don't you?"

Weezie took a deep breath as she could feel an angry reaction to *'figuring it all out'*, *"You think so?"*

"Sure, we have it under control, don't we?"

"You mean me?" she paused, then *"There are still some questions that I need to find the answers to and some clarifications."*

"Yes?"

"Other than Boris, of course, that's coming from you. But I want to know just who our dead so-called Detective is. What did his fingerprints show?"

"Nothing. They weren't in the batch that we received. That was one of the more interesting things. I don't know how he did that…unless someone else removed his fingerprint papers. We just never received those."

"Do you think Boris removed them?"

"Well, that is something we intend to find out when we interrogate him. Unless that logbook tells us something. If it does, please give me a call or shoot me a text, ok?"

"Certainly. Always nice to talk with you, Bud. Take great care of yourself."

"You too, Weezie. Talk soon."

Weezie thought to herself, 'Who the Hell IS this Boris? And why is he so important to them? I suppose I could let my imagination run away with it, but why do that when there is a possibility that the logbook will tell me something.' And off she went to her cabin to begin reading it.

She did find out some things from the logbook, as the so-called Detective kept fairly good notes. Except he didn't use names, he used numbers for people. For instance, she was able to figure out that 74 and 75 were the two slain women on the train. 66 sounded like it could be Boris. 65 was easy, as he called her 'tall, dark and gorgeous'…who else could it be but the one and only Natasha/Katherine/Oksmiella?

There were a few entries about #66, such as 'he didn't have the appearance I expected him to have'; 'he talks so quietly when we are meeting, as if he suspects someone is listening in', and '#66 will be giving me a bonus for something I really don't want to do. I was hired to follow and watch, not to take this kind of action. But $10,000 is a lot of money, and I sure could use it.'

Suddenly, Weezie felt as if she may have put together this crazy puzzle and had to sit back in her seat or she might have fallen out of it. *"Oh, my God!"* she blurted out. *"I have been so blind. How could I not have figured this out?!"*

Then her phone *'tweeted'* again, and she saw it was Guy. Back to the bathroom down the hall.

"Hey there, Weezie, how are you doing out there?" he sounded so light-hearted, quite the opposite of the way she was feeling.

"Guy, I think I have just figured something out, but I won't say anything until I am sure. What do you have for me?"

"Sure, I am fine, thank you for asking."

"Oh, sorry, I have been reading through Pinkton's logbook, trying to decode it. Strange man."

"Yeah, from what you have shared with us, you had a feeling about him from the beginning. So, was he as shady as you suspected?"

"Yes, I think he was. And I also think he was working for Boris. Now I have to figure out Boris's part in all of this. I have a suspicion, but I want to be sure."

"Well, I don't have any good news for you, which is why I called instead of waiting until tonight or texting. I wanted to tell you how sorry I am that the social media search pulled up absolutely nothing."

"Ah, not surprised. Just kind of goes along with the rest of my day so far."

"I called in a friend of mine, a real techie, and he says that the girl's accounts were pulled from all social media. He said that there are what he calls 'shadows' of her accounts, but they have been hidden or killed for some reason. Probably because she was working for the government. You know how the government is…really secretive about these things. And they have the power

to do that. At least that's what he said to me. And he would know."

Weezie sighed, wishing it was all solved and over. She was getting a stress headache again. Time for more coffee. *"Not your fault, Guy. Thanks for trying, I appreciate that."*

"Anything for you, Weezie. I hope your day improves. I can tell from your voice, you're a bit down."

"Way down." They signed off and she left the bathroom to find the others in the dining room. It was time for their meeting.

CHAPTER 23

HOW & WHY?

"You're not defined by your past; you're prepared by it. You're stronger, more experienced, and you have greater confidence."
- Joel Osteen

The dining room was empty except for an older couple enjoying their late afternoon tea and conversation. At the other end of the room was the table where they usually met. Millie was already there, talking quietly with the two FBI agents. As Weezie walked towards them, she felt someone behind her. It was Passer, who had come to join them. She smiled at him, and they continued to the table together.

Millie looked up, greeting them, *"There you are, Weezie. Did you have a chance to read the logbook? And Hello, Passer, nice to see you again."*

Weezie and Passer nodded and sat down, just as both of their stomachs made loud grumbling noises. *"Oh, my. You must be hungry,"* as Millie looked at the others, *"Why don't I go to the kitchen and see if I can find something for us?"*

As she stood to leave, Weezie asked her, *"Where is Bitsy?"*

"Oh, my dear, Bitsy is resting. You know her. I actually think that she gets bored quickly at our table talk. It has now become quite beyond her comprehension. I think she had been joining us before when it was proving to be more interesting, more

questions, and she could keep up with us. The poor dear." And with that, Millie headed to the kitchen.

The group made some small talk until she returned with a huge tray of sandwiches for them, setting it in the middle of their table. Then a couple of the kitchen staff came in with water for them, offering to get them some coffee, which they all agreed would be a good idea. It seemed that all of the thinking they had been doing was aided by lots of coffee.

"So, Weezie, how goes the logbook reading? Find out anything interesting?" asked Willis.

Weezie filled them in on what she had found out, what the numbering system was for, and the little bits that she was able to figure out. *"I just don't get it. Who did he think was going to look at his logbook? Why did he feel he had to code everything in numbers? And I think he did a rather bad job of that. I had no trouble figuring out who was who, at least for this case. I didn't look at any of the previous pages that weren't pertinent, just skimming over them."*

"Numbers? What the heck? That's a bit strange, isn't it? Especially when it was so easy for you to figure it out." Willis looked at the others, *"I get the impression he wasn't all that smart of a guy. He certainly didn't impress me when I first met him. Quite slovenly and ill kept, if I may say."* They all nodded in agreement.

"But I wonder why Boris hired him to watch over the two women? And the bonus…was that for him to then kill them? Pinkton didn't seem to want to do that part, although the money did tempt him." Weezie was thinking out loud, *"Did he indeed kill them?"*

Passer joined in, *"And who exactly IS this Boris? He seems like quite the shyster to me."* And he turned to Agent Mather, *"Are you guys going to interrogate him soon? He is getting extremely restless and loud. All he does is yell out to us and complain, while stomping his feet."*

Millie looked serious as she shared a thought, "*If Pinkton wanted that bonus money so badly, why didn't he then hide it somewhere in his luggage or briefcase after he got it? Why was it just sitting there, loose in his pocket? It just made it so obvious.*"

"*Hmm, yes, I was thinking about that too, Millie,*" commented Weezie. "*I get the feeling that when he was killed, the money was then stuffed into his pocket to show us all that he did, indeed, kill the women and was paid handsomely for it. It was almost a set-up, but a waste of money if you think about it. Why pay him after you kill him?*"

"*Ah, to cinch the case, as it were,*" added Passer, who seemed to be actually enjoying all of this conjecturing. "*I think there was a choice not to pay him, since he was now dead, but that the money in his pocket would then show his guilt. Very interesting…but wait! Who killed Pinkton?*"

"*Oh, I think there is no mystery about that,*" said Weezie. "*It was Boris, of course. Isn't it obvious? He was the one who hired Pinkton, first to watch the women, then to kill them. What do you think,*" as she turned to Willis.

"*It does certainly seem to add up. We have a lot to talk about with Boris,*" and then Willis's cell phone rang. "*Hang on a minute, it's my boss,*" as he stood and walked away from the table.

Everyone sat and looked at one another, grabbed a sandwich and dug in while Willis was on the phone. He was too far away from them to hear his conversation, so they decided to fill the time with filling their stomachs.

Willis got off the phone, then signaled to Mather to join him, away from the table. When they returned a few minutes later, they both looked serious. Willis looked over at Weezie, "*Looks like I will be taking Boris to headquarters for the interrogation.*" Then he looked at Passer, "*The helo will be here within fifteen minutes to take us to the plane. Can you come with me, Passer, so we can fill out your paperwork to release him to my care?"*

With one last look over at Weezie, Willis walked away from the table with Passer, who wore a look of confusion. They all felt a bit confused by this. '*Why did they need to take Boris to FBI headquarters?'* Weezie looked over at Mather, who said, "*Okay, Weezie, we need to talk,"* and as he stood, "*Would you all excuse us please*?"

As he walked ahead of her, Weezie looked back at Millie, and they both shrugged their shoulders.' *One thing, though,'* thought Weezie, '*Now I get some answers.'*

CHAPTER 24

ANSWERS FROM THE FEDS

"It is our choices that show what we truly are,
far more than our abilities."
- J. K. Rowling

Agent Mather led the way to Weezie's cabin, where they sat face to face. She waited for him to begin. He cleared his throat, *"Well, Weezie, it is time we shared the answers to all of your questions. Bud apologizes, as do I, for not being totally straight with you before, but we needed everything to be verified."*

She leaned towards him, *"First, can you tell me about Pinkton? His fingerprints had been missing so it was difficult to tell exactly who he was. Did they solve that question?"* It was so typical of Weezie to take the lead. There were some things she just didn't have the patience for, and that was secrets kept from her.

"Yes, he has proven to be the seedy character he claimed to be. I mean, he was basically a 'Detective For Hire', and the Ruizinho family did just that. They wanted to watch the two women, see where they went, who they talked to. He didn't figure out who they actually were until you told him. Then he realized that he didn't kill the real wife and daughter, but imposters. And we think he felt that his life was in danger if Boris found out."

She nodded, *"Ah, so it was Boris who hired him, as I thought."*

"Yes, it was Boris. We have confirmed just exactly who Boris is using the fingerprints from this case. We have an agent

under cover within the Ruizinho crime family, who has been feeding us information. It looks like Akim Ruizinho quietly disappeared about a year and a half ago. And Boris appeared about the same time, all covered with long hair and beard, difficult to see his actual features. But the eyes and the fingerprints don't lie. Our under-cover agent confirmed it too. If you look at pictures of Ruizinho, you can see his large, dark, intense eyes. If you compare them with Boris, you see those same eyes."

Weezie leaned back in her seat, "Aha, so what I suspected was true. Boris IS Akim Ruizinho. Hiding in plain sight."

"You knew?"

"I suspected as much. So, Boris/Akim needs to be back at FBI headquarters for two cases…the Ruizinho trial as well as for murdering Pinkton. Very clever."

"Boris did try to make it look as if Pinkton was paid well to kill the women, which he was, just posthumously. The thing he didn't think much about was that we would figure it out and then look for Pinkton's killer. I don't know what he thought we would do, just let it go? It seems that he would have tried to set someone else up for that murder. Sorry, Weezie, just thinking out loud."

"So, Boris/Akim hoped that the case of Pinkton's murder would be closed before they figured out who he really was. But, I agree, he left that big loose end…who else was supposed to have killed Pinkton? Do you think he would have indicated Oksmiella?"

"Even Oksmiella didn't know who Boris really was. And it also looks like Boris actually DID fall for her. She has made a statement already, and we have moved her onto the other case against the Sidorov family. She is a very smart woman, and I think she will be a great help in that case…as long as she holds it together and doesn't decide to just kill the man. She does get rather emotional when she talks or even thinks about her sister. I really wouldn't blame her, but we have to keep reminding her that the man and his syndicate have a lot to pay for, more than her *sister's death."*

"What about the REAL Ruizinho wife and daughter? Are they safe somewhere?"

"Yes, we have moved them again. We also have tried to make them look a bit different, you know, hair dye, that sort of thing. They will be safe until the trial starts."

"When will that be?"

"We have the case ready to go, so within a week or so. We have been preparing for this for years. Now that we have Boris/Akim, we can get started. We WILL give him a chance to tell us what happened, plus turn state's evidence, but I doubt he will want to do that. He is a strong, stubborn man, who is actually very proud of all that he has done. You know, the poor immigrant story, and how he rose to be so rich, and on and on."

"Thank you, Agent, for telling me all of this. Can I fill in Millie and Bitsy too? And Passer? Or is it too early for me to do that?"

"No, go ahead. I know that you all know how important it is to keep what you know under wraps. And I'm sure you are used to that, right?"

Weezie smiled and nodded. She couldn't wait to see their faces as they react to the story of Boris/Akim. And Oksmiella. Weezie felt how proud she was of that woman, how she turned something that wasn't what she thought it was into something that was. Now, she can go after the right crime syndicate to avenge her sister's death.

CHAPTER 25

FAKE EVERYTHING

'Your image isn't your character. Character is what you are as a person."
- Derek Jeter

After eating dinner that night, the three gals went to Weezie's cabin to call back home to Crip and Guy. They made sure to wait until it was after dinner back East, then called excitedly.

And Bitsy was the first one to shout into the phone, "*Guess what?! The case is solved here! Isn't that exciting?!*"

Weezie and Millie laughed, then explained to both Crip and Guy what they had learned from. Crip and Guy stayed quiet until the end when Bitsy jumped back in, "*Wow, what a case! Right? Russian mobsters and everything! And three murders.*"

Guy was the first to comment, laughingly, "*Yes, Bitsy, very exciting! Now, Weezie and Millie, when did you suspect that Boris wasn't who he pretended to be?*"

Millie and Weezie looked at one another, and Millie responded, "*Well, I think it was Weezie who actually was the first to suspect just who Boris might be. When was that?*"

"*Well, I guess it was when I was talking with Bud at the FBI, and there were some missing fingerprints, namely Pinkton's. But he didn't mention that Boris's were missing, so I had assumed that they were a part of the package sent to him. The way he was talking about it, I knew that there was something that he wasn't sharing with me. Mostly about Boris. And when the FBI agents here mentioned to me, I can't remember which one said it, but I was told that they were 'after Boris.' It made me think why and then I figured that he must be a big part of something that was going on, in connection with the Ruizinho case. And then it connected in my mind, but I still wasn't positive, just considering that he may be connected to Akim in some way. It was later when I suspected that maybe he WAS Akim, but I couldn't tell anyone until the right moment. Guy, you told me once to 'Look for the missing piece or the piece that doesn't fit with the rest of the puzzle, remember? There were several 'missing pieces' to this case. And when I was thinking about who Boris really was, I decided he was THE missing piece, or the 'misfit' piece. And his being Akim made the most sense to me."*

"And that's when you heard from the FBI agent that he was indeed the same person…Akim was Boris, I mean Boris was Akim." Crip started laughing, "*I can't believe that he had two identities and his girlfriend had three…Natasha, Katherine and Oksmiella. Talk about faking…*"

"*Yes, Crip, you are right. This case had so many fake people in it, which really can make it hard to solve.*" Weezie had to pause a moment and collect her thoughts. "*Firstly, the two women that Millie noticed, mother and daughter. They were not who they were supposed to be. They were supposed to be Alina and Sofia Ruizinho. Instead, they were Susan and Meredith Brown.*"

"*And Detective At Large Pinkton was actually a Detective For Hire, like we thought,*" added Bitsy.

"*Yes, good point, Bitsy. But instead of being a fake, he was just a guy who could be bought. He still was Pinkton, just that he was a rat instead of a man.*" And Weezie laughed again with the rest of them.

"*The only good rat is a dead one,*" added Bitsy.

"*Well done, girl,*" commented Millie. More laughter. "*And don't forget the under-cover FBI agent on the train. She was a fake too."*

"Well, are we forgetting anyone?" asked Guy.

"No, I don't think so. I think we have named all of the fakes in this case. There were 5 with fake names and 1 who wasn't really who he said he was. So, let's call him a fake too." Weezie lost it again, crying as she sat back laughing. *"I wonder what is next with this case."*

"Are we done with it?" asked Millie.

"Unless we need to testify to anything, I think so. But," added Weezie, "I wonder what the ending will be when all is said and done. We will need to keep track of it in the papers."

"I sincerely hope they don't put your names in any of the stories," said Crip. "We might need to hire security guards for you."

"That would be my job," added Guy.

They ended the call that night with a lot of laughs and relief that it was over. The train would be on the way again in the morning, and life would return to normal for the three ladies from Upstate New York.

CHAPTER 26

RELIEF FINALLY

"Sometimes you can't see yourself clearly until you see yourself through the eyes of others."
- Ellen DeGeneres

Weezie, Millie and Bitsy had a chance to say goodbye to the two policemen from Bahrump Junction, Nevada early the next morning. The FBI was long gone, so it was just the five of them standing on the station platform. Passer seemed sad to see them go, *"You guys have brought the most excitement that this town has ever seen, at least in my lifetime. We will be sorry to see you go, but I know you probably want to get home."*

Weiss seconded his cousin's comments, *"You probably already guessed that not much goes on in this small town. We deal with a death once in a while, but it is usually natural."* He looked over at Passer, *"Except for that one time a guy that had gotten really drunk, broke his beer bottle over the counter and used it to stab his best friend to death. Remember that? The poor guy couldn't remember a thing the next morning, and just couldn't believe that he had killed his best friend."*

Bitsy seemed fascinated by this, *"What happened to him?"*

Passer looked down at his feet, *"Well…he was sent to prison for life. But he couldn't live with himself, so it wasn't long before he hanged himself with the sheets in his cell."* Then he looked back up, *"Saddest thing to ever happen here."*

Bitsy had tears in her eyes, *"I'm so sorry to hear that story. Did you know him well?"*

Passer and Weiss looked at one another, then Passer answered her, *"Yeah, he was our cousin. You probably also guessed that we are all pretty much related here. Small towns are like that, you know? Or at least, we all know one another like family. That was the saddest thing to happen, and my father is the one who had to take him to jail. We were still in training when that happened. But we'll never forget it."*

On that sad note, the three elder ladies hugged the two young men as if they were related too, long and hard squeezes. It looked as if the two policemen would begin to cry, so the ladies said their goodbyes, thanked them for their help, and got back on the train.

As soon as the train pulled away from the station, the gals sat down in the dining room and pulled out their train itinerary, as they didn't want to miss anything on the rest of their journey.

After they left Nevada, the train made its way through Salt Lake City, Utah with its gorgeous scenery and interesting Mormon heritage. Unfortunately, the train was so behind schedule, they didn't stop there, as they would have normally. The gals did have the option of jumping off there and spending a day or two, then catching the next train, but they were pretty tired and decided to simply sit back and look out the window.

They had heard that the journey between Utah and Colorado was regarded to be the most spectacular train ride in all of the U.S. It was fun looking out the window at the *'American Wild West'*, the astonishing southern rim of the Book Cliffs, and into Colorado, by the sign *'Utah-Colorado'* painted on the wall of Ruby Canyon straddling the two states. They spent hours witnessing the Rocky Mountains and through the beautiful Colorado canyons. They noticed that much of their journey through Colorado was following the path of the Colorado River, along with the odd breed of Colorado wildlife indigenous to the area.

Weezie had thought to bring binoculars, and the gals spent a lot of their time fighting over them. *"The country is just so beautiful,"* commented Bitsy, at one point, with another one of those far-away looks on her face. The other two gals were happy that she was enjoying herself. It probably made up for all of those boring days spent in the small town in the middle of nowhere.

Denver was one of the highlights of this stretch of the trip for the gals, indeed, a very *'high'* location on a mountain, just outside of the Mile High City, overlooking the vast flatlands.

After that, they quickly went through four states, from Colorado, through Nebraska, Iowa and to Illinois, where they mainly slept through the night.

"Have you ever been to Chicago, Weezie?" asked Bitsy the next morning as they walked up the stairs at the Union Station.

Before Weezie could answer, Bitsy continued, *"I was in a play here once. It was an 'off Broadway' play that never got to 'on Broadway', but it was fun. And of course, I had a bunch of admirers at my door afterwards. I could sing and dance really well back in those days,"* and a far-away look came over her face. They saw that look on her face a lot…could have meant many things, such as lost in thought, in memories, or just being Bitsy…ditsy.

"Fond memories, huh, Bitsy?" asked Millie.

A sad look came over Weezie's face as she shared. *"Well, I did have a case that took me to Chicago many years ago. My husband Earl and I were involved in a murder case, trying to pull together the facts for the prosecuting attorney. It was a tough one, one of our toughest. But we did the job and they got 'their man' so to speak. Not good memories for me, but it could be called an adventure, I guess."*

"Why, Weezie?" asked Millie.

"Why what?"

"I mean, why didn't it have good memories for you?"

"Someday I might tell you that story, but not right now. We do get a few hours to spend in the 'windy city', so let's get a plan together, ladies." And so they did.

When they walked off the train, true to its name, Chicago almost *'blew them away'*. When they were standing next to the lighthouse, the three gals looked at one another and said in unison, *"Bad hair day!"* They managed to do quite a bit, taking pictures of each of them standing beside the outdoor dinosaur, and finding interesting underwater creatures at the John G. Shedd Aquarium. Bitsy was *'talking'* with one of the seals and he blew a mouthful of water on her. Best picture of the day!

They were coming out of one of the candy stores that Bitsy insisted they stop at, when they realized they would need to hurry and get to the train before it left. By the time they arrived at the station, it was REALLY a bad hair day. They ended that adventure with a lot of laughs. Always a great way to end a day.

The train traveled through Illinois, Indiana, Ohio and Pennsylvania before entering New York State. As soon as they saw the Hudson River, Bitsy began hopping up and down in her seat, *"We're almost home, ladies! And we just crossed America by train! What an adventure!"*

Millie and Weezie sat and smiled, watching this 70+ but still young lady act like she was perhaps 12 or 13.

Yes, it was an epic 3,397-mile journey across America, through 11 states and 4 time zones in what would have been four days but turned into almost a week. *'They'* say that traveling by train gives you a glimpse into the *'soul of America'*. Weezie felt like she had glimpsed too many additional *'souls'* on this trip. She just wanted to get back home. As she looked at the other two gals, she could tell that they were ready too.

CHAPTER 27

SECOND ACT ?

"There are no mistakes, only opportunities."
- Tina Fey

The gals were all packed into their car for the drive home after seeing the rest of the country from Chicago to New York City. Millie took the wheel to drive them back upstate to Rochester, and wondered out loud, *"I wonder how Oksmiella is doing. Weezie, do you think we could check in with the FBI and see if they need anything else from us? And perhaps find out how Oksmiella is? I feel as if we were instrumental in getting her back on the right track. And,"* as she looked over at Weezie, who was sitting shotgun, *"I sort of feel, I guess, sort of responsible for her, you know? Towards the end, she seemed like just such a lost soul, don't you think?"*

Weezie smiled at her friend, who wanted to be a mother or grandmother to just about everyone she met, *"Yes, I can call Bud. We will find out about her. I trust my friends at the FBI. I'm sure Mather and Willis are watching out for her. But I'll call anyway, just to ease our minds. Okay?"*

"Okay, I appreciate that. Can I be on the call with you?"

"Me too?" chimed in Bitsy from the backseat.

"Of course," said Weezie with a smile. *"You were a part of all of this too. We will do a joint call, and include Crip and Guy, too. How does that sound?"*

Both girls smiled back and nodded.

The rest of the drive back was filled mostly with small talk, about some of the scenery they had seen, even the wine they had tasted back in California.

"Do you think our wine cases will arrive okay, Weezie?" asked Bitsy, who does love her wine.

"I'm sure it is already here, Bitsy. What do you say to opening a bottle to celebrate when we get back home?"

"Weezie, that's a great idea," agreed Millie, who loves a glass once in a while.

The gals couldn't believe how everyone was so happy they were back, so full of questions like, *"Wow, what an adventure you had on your train. Are you going to write a book about it?"* was one of the most common ones from others who lived in their apartment tower the *'High Towers'* at the Highland Senior Facility.

Crip and Guy were waiting at their usual dining table, trying to contain their excitement. But when they saw the gals come into the room, Guy had to get up and hug each one, *"Welcome home, dear ladies! We missed you! Come sit and relax."*

And Crip joined in with *"We have one of the bottles of wine you sent from California, ready to open and make a toast to your return from what I would call a VERY interesting adventure."*

Everyone laughed as they enjoy a glass of wonderful California Chablis, along with a few moans because it tasted so good. *"Oh, ladies, how I wish I could have been there and tasted all of these amazing crushed grapes,"* exclaimed Crip. She was someone who also enjoyed drinking wine with her nightly meal.

The laughter continued through dinner. Over desert, Weezie asked them, *"Would you like to join me in calling the FBI Director Bud to ask for an update on the case, as well as check in with Oksmiella?"*

"*What a wonderful idea,*" commented Crip, as she began pushing her wheelchair back from the table. Guy smiled at the others as he tapped Crip on the shoulder and took over driving her. "*Where to ladies?*"

"*How about my apartment?*" suggested Weezie. "*I get very good reception there, and we can have another glass of wine.*"

Nods all around as they left the dining room for the elevator.

Weezie called Bud up on his cell phone. "*Good evening, Weezie. And I suppose everyone is there with you? Good evening, all.*"

Weezie got right to the point, "*Bud, we were thinking we would love to hear how things on this case are going. And we can't seem to get Oksmiella out of our heads. I guess you could say we are a bit worried about her. She went through a lot, especially when she learned that she was going after the wrong Russian syndicate.*"

"*Well, then, let me tell you what is going on,*" But said with a bit of a chuckle. "*I love how you ladies, and Guy of course, get so involved with the adventures you seem to find yourself in.*"

"*To start, the Ruizinho syndicate trial starts in a few weeks. We have all of the testimonies we need. And thank you ladies for giving us yours. Don't you love this modern technology called video taping, where we can actually get interviews that stand up in court without having people be at the trial in person?*"

"*We were happy to do it, Bud. So, things are progressing all right for the trial. A quick question about Boris/Akim. Which one does he look like now? Is he still acting like Boris, or did he get a shave and a haircut to be the real Akim again?*"

"*He is Akim again. We do have him on video too, though, where he was acting like Boris, before we told him we knew who* he really was. Then, he broke down and admitted everything. I think he was just too darned tired of pretending anymore. I hope he doesn't rescind it all when he is on the stand. At least, if his lawyers put him on the stand. They may decide not to. We won't know until it all starts."

"Bud, how about Oksmiella? How is she doing? And what exactly IS she doing now?" Weezie felt Millie's hand on her arm, and could sense the concern her friend had for the poor girl who was caught up in the wrong kind of spying.

"She is doing GREAT!" Bud almost shouted it. "She is so amazing, very intelligent, and is following all the protocols and doing her job as a new special agent. We had to make her title a 'special agent' because she, for now, is just on this one case. And she has another name too. Let's see, how many names is that..four?"

Millie couldn't help herself, "This is Millie, Bud. I am concerned about her. Exactly what is she doing now. And is she in any danger at all?"

Bud chuckled again, "No, Millie. We have undercover agents protecting her. She has already gotten herself accepted into the Sidorov syndicate. She seems to be quite a natural at this." He paused, "But of course, you realize there is no way you guys can get in touch with her. Remember, she is undercover."

Weezie couldn't help but react, "We understand. And she has a rather personal reason to be spying on them. They were the ones, after all, who killed her sister and her sister's boyfriend. When do you think that case will be ready to finish?"

"Weezie, you know I have no answer to that. But we do hope it won't be too long. She has already gotten us some very damaging information against them. I don't think it will be much longer, maybe a couple of months or so. At least, that is what I hope, at this point in time."

"Thank you, Bud, and I'm sure that you are taking good care of her. Would it be okay if we checked in with you from time to time and see how she is doing?" asked Weezie.

"I would love for you to do that. That would also help me keep tabs on you, Weezie, and your friends of course. And what is it you call yourself? Ah, yes, the Cackle Gang. I love it!" And he laughed so hard, tears escaped from his eyes. It was a good way to release tension at the end of a long tedious FBI day.

"Ladies, I need to go. But thank you for the call. Somehow, I always feel better after talking with you, especially you, Weezie. You and I have a history, and I want to stay in closer touch than we have been doing."

"Me, too, Bud. Take great care of yourself. And please, if anything happens that you would like me, or us, know about, give me a call."

"Happy to. Goodnight ladies, and gentleman," another laugh as he signed off.

CHAPTER 28

WELL, THAT'S A SURPRISE!

"Don't cry because it's over, smile because it happened."
- Dr. Seuss

It was about two months later when Millie opened the newspaper and gasped. *"Oh, my God!"* She immediately texted the other gals and Guy to meet downstairs in the dining room. She had something important to show them.

When they were all together, sitting and sipping coffee, Millie pulled out the newspaper and opened it. And she began reading, *"Never has this reporter seen such an event in our courts as what happened today. Everyone was seated, as the audience had been allowed in, consisting of curiosity seekers, Russian family members, the press, and others. Things went quiet. The court called up to the stand, Akim Ruizinho's estranged wife Alina. She was dressed all in black, signifying what exactly? Perhaps the end of their marriage, or perhaps the end of the syndicate? She seemed very composed and kept looking over at her daughter Sofia who was sitting in the first row behind the Ruizinho family lawyers. There was something other than calm on her young face, perhaps fear? Or perhaps stoic certainty? But she and her mother held their gazes. Ah, yes, perhaps determination. Both were anxious to testify against Akim. When the first question was posed to Alina Ruizinho, she began by pointing at her husband, ranting accusations at him, that it was ''all his fault' for ruining their family, ruining their lives...with his greed and his cruelty to people.' She then clutched her cross that was hanging around her neck, and she added, 'He is guilty of all that you say. And he is guilty of going against God with murder and unspeakable crimes. May the*

Devil welcome him.' And with that, she reached inside her purse and brought out a gun. She pointed at him and shot him once in the forehead. Then she sat down, very composed as she placed the gun on the railing in front of her."

Millie looked up at everyone, then back down at the paper, continuing, "*The crowd went berserk. There was so much yelling, the judge was banging his gavel calling for order, the defense attorneys were checking to see if Ruizinho was dead or not. This reporter wonders how she was able to get that gun past the check-in x-ray machines. One of the prosecutors went over to grab the gun with his handkerchief, and we all could see that it looked like it was made from a 3D printer or maybe of ceramic.*

"*And yes, Akim Ruizinho was dead. She got her wish…he would meet the Devil. What an end to a criminal case that has spanned several years in preparations and evidence gathering. I have to say that this reporter is stunned by this development. I could see the daughter rise and calmly walk back through the crowd to the back of the courtroom. Should she be stopped? Was she in on this with her mother? What the Hell happened here? And we wonder now what?*"

Millie looked up again at the others, who had stunned looks on their faces. She looked back down at the paper, "*I just can't believe this! So, Boris/Akim is dead? He won't pay for what he has done in his criminal life? How can something like this happen?*"

Weezie reached over and placed her hand on Millie's "*My dear, who knows how something like this can happen. But at least the mother and daughter of a crime syndicate king have gotten their revenge. I guess it might be called a 'fitting end' to the man's criminal career. I don't know really what else to say.*"

Guy cleared his throat, "*One thing I do know is that now that poor woman, the wife, is going to jail for killing her rat of a husband. How can that be okay? And will the daughter be sent to* jail too? For conspiracy to commit a murder?"

Millie added, "*It is just so unfair! The man got what he deserved...death. But now, his poor innocent wife has to pay for killing him? And what will happen to the syndicate? Will someone else step into his shoes and run it now? Or will it fall apart?*"

Bitsy had tears running down her face, "*And what about Oksmiella? Didn't she care about Boris/Akim?*"

Weezie put her other hand over Bitsy's, "*No, I don't think so, Bitsy. Oksmiella told me that she didn't care anything for that man. He was simply a means to an end for her. What I hope now is that she will be careful what she does about the real crime family that killed her sister. I hope she doesn't feel that she needs to take drastic measures like Alina Ruizinho did...kill the man who ruined their lives. Dear God, I hope she reads this in the paper and figures out she doesn't want to do that.*"

Weezie rose from her chair, "*Thank you Millie, for giving us this news. I had not had a chance to read the paper yet, I jumped right into the puzzles as I had slept in a bit this morning and missed breakfast. I think I should give Bud a call.*" Then she sat back down, "*On the other hand, what could he tell me anyway.*"

Millie sighed as she sipped her drink. "*Well, at least it's over. It is over for that poor young girl who had such a horrible father. And she is old enough perhaps to deal with her mother being taken away from her. I sincerely hope they don't connect her to what her mother did. I'm sure, she will tell everyone that her daughter had nothing to do with it. As long as that reporter drops his thoughts of her involvement, she should be all right.*" As she looked over at her friends, "*As a mother, I'm sure that her daughter's life has already been preplanned. Even if she too was involved in the plan to shoot Akim, she will be okay. After all, look at what she has been through just living in a crime family, then hiding for so long, being taken from place to place away from anyone who could get to her and her mother to kill them. Yes, I'm sure she will be just fine. I bet you anything that she will disappear. That's what I would do. What do you think?"*

Guy was the one to answer that question. *"If she is smart, and I'm sure she is, she will do exactly that. I'm sure that her mother was able to stash away some funds so that her daughter could start a new life. After living in a crime family all those years, she probably learned a thing or two about how to do that."* He sighed, *"Yes, I'm sure she will be just fine."*

And he rose from the table, *"Back to work for me, ladies, making sure all is secure and safe here. That case is over."* He smiled at them and left the room.

- **THE END** -

AUTHOR'S NOTE

Thank you for choosing to read *The Faces of Murder*. This is the second in the Hightower Mysteries Series. I wanted to give you a few clarifications and tell you where my ideas came from for the main characters.

The nursing care facility that the four gals live in is a fictional facility that came from my memories of my great-grandmother, who lived in one there in Rochester, N.Y., near Highland Park. I don't know if it is still there or not. I took that idea and expanded on it, adding in a critical care facility for those who needed constant care, while also providing needed medical services to those living in the adjoining '*High Towers*'. Yes, in the story, Weezie Hightower's husband's family was very wealthy and bequeathed enough money to build the Towers. Three of the gals live there while Crip lives in the care facility due to being a paraplegic. In one of the upcoming books, we will learn her story as we will learn more about each one of these four ladies.

Characters in any of my fictional stories are conglomerations of the many people in my life that I have met over the years. The names are fictional for each of them. Weezie is based on my mother, with a mixture of personality traits, some being hers, some mine, and some from other people. Mom's last name was not Hightower. Crip was based on an actual person who was a member of her Cackle Gang, which was a real group of Mom and some of her friends back in the 40s and 50s. Crip in the story is different from the real Crip, but yet I have kept her warm personality. I remember her hearty laugh and positivity, which I have pulled into our fictional Crip. The real Crip was not in a wheelchair.

The other two gals in the Gang, Bitsy and Millie are from my imagination. I wanted four gals who were completely different in history and personality, who met at Highland Park Facility and who '*clicked*'. Bringing in their variety of personalities and life stories adds to the richness and realism of the books. These are four gals that I would love to actually meet and talk with. How enjoyable it would be to watch them interact. And so here they are, on an adventure, and I hope that they entertained you.

I have wanted to take the railroad train across this great country of ours, from New York City to California, then drive up the coast to the wine country, then either train or plane back home. Maybe one day.

And I hope that this story pulled you into this fictional world, keeping you guessing until the very end.

Marilyn AUTHOR

ABOUT THE AUTHOR

Marilyn Wright Dayton has been writing all her life, from the time she could hold a pencil. Her life and career focused on the world of advertising in many roles. She was one of the originators of some of the more unique marketing vehicles in the nation over many years. From the beginning of her career at the age of 12 as a radio quiz kid, she has been both in front of the camera and behind the camera as a fashion model, radio and TV show host and program producer, newspaper reporter, creative writer, ad director and owner (as Marilyn Wright-Schulz), entrepreneur, consultant, trainer and an authority in the areas of creative marketing and top-notch business performance. Until retirement, she was a marketing consultant and a TV host/producer.

Marilyn is now retired from the business world and makes her home with her family in Mystic, CT. Her first loves have continued to be creative writing and art. She has written and published several books of short stories, novellas, and novels on political themes and murder mysteries. Marilyn continues to plan to write books through 2025 with her list of around 15 books. After that, who knows, maybe more?

www.MarilynDayton.com
maredayt@yahoo.com

A Look Inside "Murder on the Mesa"
The Hightower Mystery Series Book 1

CHAPTER 1

A MURDER IN ARIZONA

"One always dies too soon...or too late."
- from '*No Exit*' by Jean-Paul Sartre

She lay on the ground, feeling the life seeping out of her. She thought, *"Am I dying? It feels so peaceful."* Then she remembered what had happened and she began to fight it, *"No, I can't – I have to fix this! I have to…."* But then she was gone, with her beautiful but blank eyes staring up at the blue Arizona sky. No more life in her young, sweet body, so full of life and promise only seconds ago.

Her horse Brandy watched her, not knowing what to do. She loved this girl and had always been there for her, through innocent and painful tears, to joyous laughter when life had become happier for her.

And now that girl lay on the ground, lifeless, gone forever. Brandy could feel her tears fall as she carefully lay down next to the girl to protect her from more pain in the hot Arizona sun. Brandy felt something inside her die too as she leaned over to gently slip the girl's long blonde hair between her lips one last time.

She would die for this girl – and maybe she will if no one finds them soon.

The dead girl had no idea how complicated things would get because of her '*murder*' where the Hopi & Navajo lands bordered with her father's Arizona ranch land. Her death would stoke a fire between her father and the Indian Nations about law enforcement rights and cause old wounds to reemerge from several people's pasts, pitting mother against father, friend against friend, law officer against law officer, and an elderly retired Private Investigator against her past friends and foes.

CHAPTER 2

TWO DAYS EARLIER

"A friend may well be reckoned the masterpiece of nature."
- from *'Friendship'* by Ralph Waldo Emerson

The retired Private Investigator had been packing and decided to join her friends for one last get together to play cards, followed by lunch, before leaving for Arizona. Louise *'Weezie'* Hightower was in her early 70s, though she didn't look it. She lived in the Hightower apartments beside the Highland Park Clinic in Rochester, New York. Her late husband's family was wealthy and had left money to the Clinic to build the *'Hightowers'*, two tall buildings (that look like silos), with senior residential facilities for those who needed living quarters near a medical facility.

She was late, but only by a few minutes. Yet, the other three gals looked up with some slight irritation in their eyes, mixed with a touch of sadness. As usual, Bitsy was the first to open her mouth, *"You're late, Weezie. How can we get our two hours of card playing in if you are late?"* Bitsy had a tendency to act like a little girl, all dramatic and flighty with her hands going all over the place. This was nothing new for her. You get used to it over time, expecting her to act that way.

Weezie smiled at the three gals who had become her best friends since she arrived at this facility two years before. She had become the natural leader of their little group, and every Wednesday she led them in *'story day'*, when she shared past detective adventure stories from her days running the Hightower Detective Agency with her husband Earl. They had spent decades traveling all over the country investigating and solving cases. That's a lot of stories.

This was not a Wednesday, so they were going to play cards. It was a quarter past 10 in the morning (15 minutes late), and Bitsy grabbed the cards and began shuffling with flourish. Always with flourish, and she did it well.

Weezie wondered why everyone seemed a little '*off*'. Bitsy answered before Weezie could ask, *"You're leaving us for a whole week. In two years, you have never left our group. Why couldn't we at least go with you?"* Pout.

Weezie smiled, *"But I'll be working all the time, covering for Jake while he's gone. And I don't know what type of crimes I may walk into."*

Bitsy, ever the dramatic one, whined and said, *"Why couldn't someone else cover for him? Why you?"*

Weezie laughed, *"Probably because I had offered to, and he won't need to pay me."* The girls still looked sad, and Crip, ever the retired schoolteacher, looked at Bitsy, *"Dear, you really need to learn to get control of yourself. It's only a week, eight days, and then she will be back before you know it."*

Bitsy, still pouting, *"Well, that is MORE than a week, you know."* Millie, always a loving grandmotherly type, leaned over and patted Bitsy's hand, *"Now, dear, we will be here with you, and we will keep you busy, you will hardly know she's gone."*

Bitsy, always needing the last word about it, *"What do we do on Wednesday? She won't be here to tell her story!"* And the beginning of tears.

Weezie thought to herself how this was going to be harder than she had thought, so she added, *"OK, I promise to take you all on my next adventure."* That seemed to satisfy them, especially when she added, *"We will start planning it when I return, how does that sound?"* Smiles all around. *"Plus, I will be calling you every day to fill you in so you can be a part of it all, OK?"* Placating done.

After a few minutes of playing, Bitsy looked up and began primping, as she saw Guy Davis walk into the room. Elizabeth "*Bitsy*" Sutton was a bit of a flirt, well, more than a bit. And at her age, with the red hair, her heavily made-up face and bad choice of too-young-for-her clothing, it looked quite ridiculous to the other girls. But you had to love her anyway. They all looked up at Guy, a retired detective, now in charge of the security at their facility. And he was their friend, stopping by every day to say "*Hi*". He had been the one who named their little group the '*Cackle Gang*'.

"*Well, well, ladies, how are you doing today?*" Guy was a tall, good-looking man with a friendly attitude, and most of the ladies in the facility '*swooned*' over him. Then he looked at Weezie, "*Still want me to take you to the airport?*"

"*Of course, I think that would be wonderful,*" said Weezie.

He pulled up a chair, sitting down with a serious look on his face, "*Weezie, I was thinking. You are going to be out there in Arizona doing detective work all by yourself. How would you like some help? Someone who could work with you, and be there to protect you just in case?*"

Weezie smiled at the thought, but then pondered just for a moment, "*Are you sure about that, Guy? I really don't know how dangerous it might be, it could be really quiet with not much going on while Jake is gone.*"

Guy laughed, "*Then we could drive around and see the sights. I know you've been there before. You could show me the highlights. It'll be like a vacation.*"

Bitsy immediately popped in, "*What? The two of you together on a vacation? Being...um, together?*"

Weezie pretended not to hear her, "*Guy, I really could use the help, especially if it does get a little bit difficult, I haven't held a gun in many years.*"

This time, Millie was the one to interrupt, *"A gun?? What do you mean, a gun? Could it get that dangerous?"*

Guy was the one who responded to her, while also looking at both Bitsy and Crip, *"Don't worry girls. It doesn't always work out to be that dangerous. But you never know. And if it does, I'll be right there with Weezie. And I know how to use a gun."*

Weezie hadn't thought about the chance of her week in Arizona including anything other than investigative work. *'Quiet'* investigating at any rate. On reflection she realized it might be a good idea to have Guy around. *"Yes, Guy. I think that would be great. Are you going to use some of your vacation time from here?"*

Guy lifted his eyebrows when he smiled, *"Already asked for it. I wasn't going to let you say no."*

Bitsy looked down at her lap, trying to hide her disappointment that it wasn't her who would be spending a week with Guy. When she sighed, everyone looked at her, and Crip decided to try to make her feel better by reaching over and taking her hand. They all knew how Bitsy was, so they needed to nip this in the bud. *"Remember Bitsy, we will be heading off on an adventure with Weezie after she gets back. While she's gone, let's start thinking of what we want to do, ok?"*

Another deep sigh, but Bitsy looked up with a weak smile, *"Yes, let's be ready with ideas when she gets back. I already have some."* And her smile widened, as she started feeling better, *"Let's eat."* No more cards, it was almost lunchtime.

The airplane trip out west proved to be fairly uneventful. Weezie and Guy got their rental car and headed to the motel in Flagstaff, where they had rooms next to one another, with an adjoining door. All the better to work together on cases.

Weezie began to feel excited. She hadn't seen her nephew Jake since he had taken over the Hightower Agency two years before. To her, giving him a week of vacation was going to be interesting, and she hoped there would be at least one case to test her.

CHAPTER 3

ONE DAY BEFORE – THE HIGHTOWER AGENCY

"The value of life lies not in the length of days, but in the use you make of them."
- by Montaigna

Early the next morning, they met with Jake at the Hightower Detective Agency offices in Flagstaff. He had taken over the business shortly after Weezie's husband Earl had died, working with Weezie until she retired. Jake seemed well suited for private investigative work, and had a full client load, as well as new, larger office space, plus a secretary. Weezie and Earl never had a need for a secretary, as they shared the workload and kept an organized office, letting their answering machine take the calls for them. Different times, different needs..

After introductions, and deep nephew-aunt hugs, they decided to talk about current cases over breakfast. They headed down the street to Jake's usual breakfast spot. Jake carried a briefcase with the paperwork he wanted to review with them.

Jake had never married, although he had come close a couple of times. It seemed none of the gals he was interested in could compare with his Aunt Weezie, someone he had always loved and admired. And in her day, she had been quite a '*dish*'.

The waitress seemed to be one of those ladies who admired Jake, as she sauntered over in her too-tight uniform and leaned towards him, "*Morning, Jake. How are you today?*" It appeared she had tunnel vision, focused only on him. Weezie looked at Guy who rolled his eyes. They sat back in the booth and waited for their turn.

"*Morning, Sally, lookin' good today.*" Yup, Jake had taken

after his Uncle Earl, all charm and charisma, with a huge smile that seemed to draw the ladies in. Weezie tried not to chuckle.

"The 'usual'?" Sally asked. Jake smiled a yes, then looked over at his breakfast guests and introduced them. *"This is my Aunt Weezie and her friend Guy. I'm sure they are hungry too, Sally."* Makes you think that if he hadn't mentioned them, Sally wouldn't have said anything to them, instead ignoring them and walking away. Again, Weezie had to hold her laughter.

After they had ordered, Weezie couldn't help herself, *"Well, Jake, I see you still have a way with the gals."* Then she allowed herself to laugh.

He looked a little embarrassed, *"Yeah, I guess that part of me related to Uncle Earl shows itself sometimes."* Smile. *"And actually, it comes in handy when I have to question people, especially the ladies….and no, I'm not dating anyone at the moment."* He looked at Guy, *"You see, there just is no one like my Aunt Weezie. No one can compare. She is adorable, still cute, smart as heck, and keeps me on my toes. I don't think there is a girl out there like her."* Then, a little sheepishly, *"I can't help it, I am asking for a lot, I know. Here I am at 38 years old, and I haven't even been engaged."*

"Does that bother you, Jake?" asked Weezie, leaning forward with concern on her face. *"I'm not here to pressure you or try to make you feel bad about it. You are the closest I ever had to a son, and you know that Earl and I have always thought of you that way."*

"I know, and I have always felt the love you both had for me. I just work all the time, and the only women I meet lately are either clients, suspects, married female cops, or…uh, Sally?" They all laughed at that.

"Don't worry, Jake, believe me, your time will come when the moment is right," added Guy. *"Trust me."*

"All right, let's get to business. What do you have for me...us?" Weezie asked as she looked over at Guy. Somehow, she knew that he would be a lot of help. Once again, she was glad he had come with her.

"Not too much that can't wait a week. Of course, that could change tomorrow. Some big case could come in, but I'm sure you have had enough of those, you could probably solve just about any case before I even come back." Jake said. *"Then, YOU will need to fill ME in."* They smiled, because it was probably true.

It didn't take too long to review just three cases that needed to be watched, and just a few inquiries to be made, fairly easy stuff for an experienced P.I. and a retired cop. One case was a robbery, where it was waiting for a police report which could come in at any time. Jake suggested that they could just add in the report to the file, give it to his secretary to hold for him, and he could handle it when he came back. No hurry there.

Another one was a wrap up and review of a case that was pretty much completed. Jake asked Weezie and Guy to look it over and if they find anything he may have missed, to check it out and prepare a report for him. The third one was just beginning. It was a murder case which happened just the week before, *"If you could review what I have, then call the police contact listed in the file, and maybe interview some of the involved parties, that would be great. Or it could wait until I return. I'm sure a few days' delay wouldn't hurt the case. I know the police have their hands full with crimes to solve and it might still take them a few days to pull together everything we would need anyway. I was trying to wrap as much up as I could to keep you from having a heavy load while I'm gone. And Janice, my secretary, is a great help. You could probably tell when you met her that she is really smart and very capable of a lot more than what a secretary usually does. Feel free to ask her anything and let her know what you need."* Then he noticed the expression on Weezie's face, *"What??"*

"Oh, nothing, honey. She seems like a real doll, cute as a

button, smart and really devoted to you and your work."

She decided to let the matter drop when she saw how red Jake's face was getting. So, she changed the subject. *"I know I have mentioned my Cackle Gang to you before, and the gals really want to feel like a part of this. Even though there isn't much in the way of activity, to them it would seem 'huge'."* She smiled, *"I love them and really want them to feel involved. You don't mind if Guy and I 'consult' them on cases, do you?"* She smiled.

Jake understood, *"Of course not. I'm sure they even wanted to come with you. Such an adventure, right?"* He smiled back. He had met the gals once and it didn't take him long to figure how they would love an adventure of any kind.

Jake continued, *"If a big case comes in, feel free to grab it and run with it. I trust you completely. And you have my cell number if you need me for anything."*

Weezie leaned in closer to him, *"No I will not call you! This is your vacation, the first in how many years? At least two years ago you took over the agency. The only time away was those few days you helped me move to Rochester. I repeat, I will NOT call you, OK?"*

They all smiled and rose from the table to go back to the office

CHAPTER 4

FINDING THE BODY

"Our dead are never dead to us, until we have forgotten them." - George Eliot

Just as she had mentally promised the girl, Brandy lay beside her for hours. The girl was Tracey Bachman, a rancher named Jack Bachman's daughter. She was young and beautiful. Tracey had been a nurse, working at the Hopi clinic, where her caring and patient personality made her popular with all who met her.

On this particular morning, her father had begun worrying about where she was. It was after noon, more than four hours after she had left for a ride. They hadn't talked much, sadly, but he knew she would have told him if she was going to be gone for hours. She was good about doing that at least. So, he began making phone calls. His first was to her cell phone, where it went to voicemail. Then he called the clinic in case she had gone there. She wasn't there.

It didn't take long before he realized that he didn't know who else to call, as he was unaware of any friends she may have had over the past couple of years. In desperation, he called his friend Anthony Musselman, the Flagstaff Chief of Police. Anthony suggested that he try to ping her phone, not promising results due to cell services being so *'spotty'* around the reservations. *"Do it, Anthony. This is just so unlike her. Do it!!"* Jack's voice reflected his desperation.

A few minutes later, Anthony called him back with good

news, "*We have her phone, just at the northern edge of your ranchland. I will pick you up and we will find her. Don't worry, Jack, we will find her. I also have sent out a team to the area to begin a detailed search. I will see you in a few minutes.*"

Jack found it painful waiting for Anthony's car, so when he saw the police car coming up his long driveway, Jack left the house quickly to meet him. That way, they could get back on the road as fast as possible. It wasn't just the hot Arizona day that caused him to sweat so profusely, it was fear, something he just couldn't shake. He had a very bad feeling about this.

It took them about 20 minutes to race across the ranch land to where they saw the other police. But they were in a cluster near the trees, not spread out searching. Had they found her?

Sadly, they had found Brandy first, then they had seen the girl lying almost under the now-dead horse. Jack had trouble climbing out of the car. He felt paralyzed. In his heart he knew she was gone when he saw the body of the horse lying so still on the ground. But he had to move closer and make sure. It was now almost five hours since she had left home.

Jack saw Tracey's long blond hair spread out on the ground beside Brandy. He fell to the ground, crawling to her, unable to see clearly through his tears. He knew she was dead. When he started to reach out to her, the police held him back, "*Jack, looks like she met someone here, and that person killed her,*" said one of the men. They pulled him back to the car, where he sat on the ground and wept, repeating her name. He had never felt so much pain. His girl. His beautiful daughter, so young. He couldn't think straight, all he could do was lean against the side of the car and weep.

Meanwhile, the police secured the scene, taking pictures before moving anything. They suspected the horse had died from exposure and heat stroke, as she had no visible wounds. But Tracey had wounds to her head. Terrible wounds. Almost half of her head had been caved in. They needed a medical examiner to see her soon and had also made calls to get a tent to set up over the bodies, to keep the bodies from deteriorating more in the hot sun.

All Jack knew was that his girl was dead. He couldn't talk at all when his friend Anthony helped lift him back into the car, until he realized they were taking him away from his girl. *"No, I need to stay with her! I can't leave her!"* Anthony tried soothing the grieving father, patiently waiting until Jack was ready to leave.

"Let's go back to the house. We need to let these men do their job. Jack, who do you want me to call? Then I need to come back here." Anthony knew the answer before Jack replied. *"No one. There is no one left."*

Over the next few hours, things got very interesting, as word spread about the girl's death. And especially where she had died, on the boundary of Jack's ranch and the American Indian lands. Soon, both the Hopi police and the Navajo police arrived to talk about jurisdiction over the investigation. If Jack had been there, he would have fought them all. As it was, Anthony did call Jack when he found that there seemed to be a problem over which police force would have precedence over the investigation.

Jack immediately lost it, *"Anthony, this is ridiculous! This is my daughter, on my land. I want you to be in charge!"*

But that was debatable to everyone concerned. He could hear the raised voices in the background. When Jack realized what was happening, he placed a call. He had heard good things about the Hightower Agency, and wanted the best, needing them to be in charge, and reporting only to him. This was his daughter! His only child! The only person he loved in this world. And his only living relative

CHAPTER 5

WEEZIE ON THE TRAIL

"It is the unknown we fear when we look upon death and darkness, nothing more."
- from *'Harry Potter and the Half-Blood* Price', J.K. Rowling

Janice was helping Weezie and Guy with their agency ID cards when the phone rang at the Hightower Agency. Judging by the look on her face, both Weezie and Guy knew something bad had happened.

"Jake is out of town, but Weezie Hightower is here. I will send her right out to meet with you at your ranch house. They will be there in 15-20 minutes. Please hold on, Mr. Bachman, we are going to try our best to help you." When she hung up, Janice turned to Weezie, *"There has been a murder and we have been hired to help solve it. Just a warning though, as this is Mr. Jackson "Jack" Bachman, a large ranch owner, the type of man who likes to be in control. But with this being his daughter, I'm sure he is feeling distraught. So be prepared for anything. Also, she was found right on the boundary of his ranch and the American Indian lands."*

Weezie was very familiar with the American Indian tribes here in Arizona. She and her husband had worked on a case for the Hopi tribe many years ago. Although she had solved it, there were some bad feelings felt by certain tribal members. But she couldn't focus on that at the moment as they had to get out to the ranch. She remembered the area where the ranch was located but couldn't recall Mr. Bachman. It had just been too many years.

She and Guy grabbed notebooks and headed out. They used their rental Jeep, selected because they had expected to have tourist time, and many of the tourist areas had rough roads. Now she was grateful for that choice, as she expected they would be going onto the reservation land during the investigation, due to jurisdiction concerns.

Guy drove, and he knew how to drive fast, from the days when he would need to get to crime scenes quickly. They arrived at the ranch house within ten minutes, record time.

When they knocked on the door, they were met by a middle-aged man whose face showed a look of deep pain, and whose slumped shoulders showed defeat. This was a man who had just lost his daughter, and Weezie wished she could reach out to him. But she would need to do it with words instead of arms.

Jack never asked about her experience but went right into explaining the circumstances. He asked them to drive him back out to the scene, where they could begin investigating. It would be difficult, he knew, but everyone at the scene would need to hear directly from him that these two people were now in charge of his daughter's murder investigation. They all would need to step back from the case and let these two take over.

Things don't always work out as planned. When they arrived, there was a battle going on, with two American Indian policemen yelling at one another and at the Flagstaff police. Anthony was the only one who understood the situation and what Jack needed and was able to quiet everyone down. They let Jack explain what he wanted them to do. It was both his land and his daughter, and Anthony felt enough respect for the man to hear him out.

That didn't mean that everyone agreed. Jack said, "*I have hired the best detective agency in the state, and they are here to lead this investigation. And I want you all to cooperate with them. For my daughter's sake.*"

So, Weezie stepped into the middle of the group, and stared at each one of them, with a look she had been known for in the past. She could quiet a group of people with that look, and she still *'had it'*.

She introduced herself and Guy, and in her best *'political'* way said, *"I understand that there is a question of jurisdiction here, so I would like to make a proposal. Why don't we ALL work on this case together. I will lead the investigation and keep you informed daily with any information I find. Please trust that I have over 50 years of experience all over the country, and I actually solved a mystery here about twenty years ago for the Hopi nation. I would like to do that again, for all of those involved. Especially Mr. Bachman. Agreed?"* Again, her look with a smile made of steel, but everyone just stared back at her. *"A nod would be fine. Even better than a handshake."* All nodded.

"All right. I would like to start by talking with the medical examiner from Flagstaff, and after the bodies are removed, I would like to go back to the ranch house with Mr. Bachman. I will begin my investigation there." She didn't wait for a response but turned to Guy and they took a closer look at the bodies. It was easy to see how much the horse must have loved the girl, using her body as a protective shield. Weezie noticed something else, motioning for Guy to follow her over for a few words with the medical examiner. She and Guy then took a few minutes to walk around the crime scene to see if they could find any clues. She did point out something to Guy but didn't say anything. She then had a quiet word with Anthony who nodded.

Everyone watched quietly, not knowing what else to do. Then Weezie and Guy walked back to the Jeep with Mr. Bachman

Look for "*Murder On The Mesa*", Book 1 in the Hightower Series, available NOW on Amazon.

OTHER BOOKS BY THE AUTHOR

"Beyond, Tales of Life, Mystery & Murder"

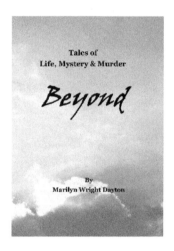

Fictional short stories from a nursing home to the Bayou, where something can happen and be a lie, another thing may not happen and seem truer than the truth. Oh, yes, there is one non-fiction one in the book.

Available on Amazon in soft cover and Kindle.

www.MarilynDayton.com

"Beyond 2, Strange But True Short Stories"

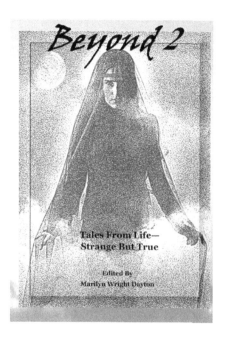

A collection of tales based on real life experiences, where the similarities are in how extraordinary the stories are.

Available on Amazon in soft cover and Kindle.

www.MarilynDayton.com

"Reflexions, Lessons Learned Along Life's Journey"

A collection of short stories, from the author's life, based on her blog From Glam 2 Gram. Stories from when she knew a young Elvis Presley, to her mentor Dick Clark, through her various adventures in radio and TV, to life.

Available on Amazon in soft cover and Kindle.

www.MarilynDayton.com

"Murder on the Mesa"

A HIGHTOWER MYSTERY, BOOK 1

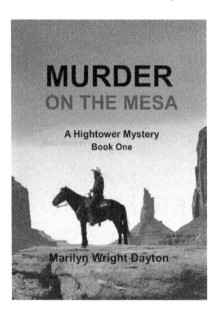

"Think Murder She Wrote, Miss Marple, Hercule Poirot - All Rolled Into One!"

This is 'edge of your seat' reading, with 'engrossing characters'. Solving crime has no age limit. Meet four ladies who are in their 70's, led by Weezie Hightower, retired Private Investigator. Weezie and Guy Davis, retired detective, head across country to Arizona, and solve a murder mystery that has SEVEN suspects. And it only takes them SEVEN days to solve it.

"Heartbreaking But Intriguing!"

Available NOW on Amazon in soft cover and Kindle.

www.MarilynDayton.com

MORE HIGHTOWER MYSTERY SERIES COMING IN 2022 THRU 2025

"Murder on Trial"

A HIGHTOWER MYSTERY, BOOK 3

"You Are My Last Hope."

A young man is on trial for murder. There are almost too many clues…what's the real story? The Hightower gals find the story confusing as they work together to solve the mystery before the verdict that would send him to his death.

COMING IN 2023
www.MarilynDayton.com

"A Question of Murder"

A HIGHTOWER MYSTERY, BOOK 4

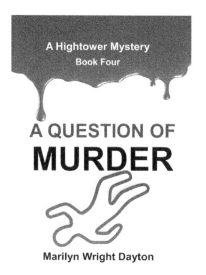

"Was it suicide or murder?"

The case is cold…VERY cold. Jake Hightower joins his aunt to help solve a case she and her late husband had worked on a couple of decades ago. There was always that question…"Was it suicide or murder?" In this riveting mystery, the second question is whether it was the first in a series of murders, and can they disprove the original claim of suicide in this reawakened crime.

COMING IN 2024
www.MarilynDayton.com

"Murder on High"

A HIGHTOWER MYSTERY, BOOK 5

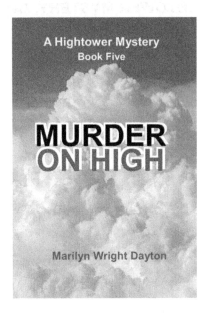

"How could this happen??"

No one expects to find dead bodies on a plane, but that is what happens to Bitsy, and her screams sound even louder up in the clouds. Bitsy and the rest of the Hightower Mysteries gals are taking a small holiday that will not end up as planned.

COMING IN 2025

www.MarilynDayton.com

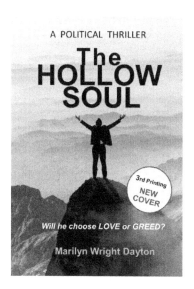

"Never Say Die"
A Guy Davis Murder Mystery Book 2

"A Who-Done-It of the Highest Order

Guy Davis comes back with his own murder mystery stories, in the years before the Hightower Mysteries. He was a detective, who followed the crime, no matter where it was.

In New Orleans, can they find out who has been killing the young women before there is another murder? When you think the case is solved, there is a complication – in the form of another dead young woman. How did that happen? How could their suspect kill another while he was locked up in their jail?

COMING IN 2024

www.MarilynDayton.com

"A Matter of Time"
A Guy Davis Murder Mystery Book 1

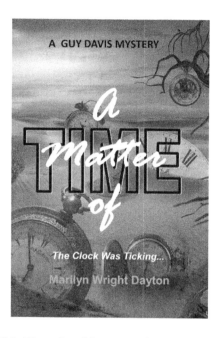

"A Murder Mystery in Detroit"

Guy Davis takes us back to a murder mystery story, from his years before the Hightower Mysteries. Guy is working with the police in Detroit this time. They have called him in as a detective who has been trained as a profiler. Here he is again living out of a suitcase. He is beginning to get used to it.

He is just beginning to pull himself together after the pain in his personal life. But he still has a long way to go. Can he concentrate on solving this case? It could just save him.

COMING SOON

www.MarilynDayton.com

"The Knowing Tree"

Marilyn Wright Dayton

"A Tree Can Talk...Telling Stories?"

"LIFE" goes on all around us and we don't usually think very much about it...in the ground, in the air, in the water, in the plant life. This is the story of one tree - a witness to history, to love, to sorrow, to death. It tell us what "she" witnesses over several centuries - how she watches, how she knows - the life of many under her protective branches, even messages written on her "skin"...

We learn about lives, wars, loves found and lost, family and friends who meet again after decades and witness their changes, but yet how they have stayed the same. We can simply read and enjoy, or we can feel the emotions, full of history, that could change our own lives

COMING IN LATE 2022

www.MarilynDayton.com

"Our Roots Run Deep",
the wRightSide Family History

Through many plastic totes of information, I was able to trace our family directly back to the days of the **Vikings**, through the **Norman Conquest, the War of 1066**, and so much more. Inside this book are included also many historical aspects that show what life was like during each time period. There is even a branch of our family that goes back to **Eric the Forester.** He was the brother of **Eric the Red**, and uncle to **Leif Ericson** (Eric's son) who originally discovered North America.

This book was published in 2020, available on Amazon.
Everyone should do genealogical research. It opens your eyes to who you really are, and how you became who you are. Fascinating. Find your ancestors. It is an amazing journey, one well worth taking.

www.MarilynDayton.com

www.wrightsidefamily.com

Made in the USA
Middletown, DE
05 March 2022